SWEET SUMMERTIDE

SARAH DRESSLER

5 PRINCE PUBLISHING
5PRINCEBOOKS.COM

Published by:

5 Prince Publishing and Books, LLC

DBA 5 Prince Publishing

PO Box 865

Arvada, Colorado 80001

Digital ISBN: 978-1-63112-405-1

Print ISBN: 978-1-63112-406-8

Cover design by Marianne Nowicki

Interior design by 5 Prince Publishing

First Edition F042225v.1

For more information about this title, visit: www.5princebooks.com

To Laura, may you forever find your own adventure and always be loved.

ACKNOWLEDGMENTS

To my children, David and Eden, for being my inspiration, my sounding boards, my critique partners, my biggest cheerleaders, and the source of so much joy, thank you.

Thank you to the love of my life, Judson, for over twenty years of adventures full of love and laughter. There are little pieces of us, encased forever, in the stories I pen. I love you.

To my friends, family, and total strangers who have become loyal readers, thank you for your constant support.

To my early readers, thank you for your valuable feedback.

To the 5 Prince Publishing team, I am grateful for all the work you do to bring my stories to life. Thank you!

ACKNOWLEDGMENTS

ALSO BY SARAH DRESSLER

CHRISTMAS COVE

Christmas Cove - Book 1

Spring Showers - Book 2

A Winter's Wedding - Book 3

Sweet Summertide - Book 4

SWEET SUMMERTIDE

CHAPTER 1

ONE MORE BUMP, A SLIGHT SHIFT OR A SHARP JOLT OF THE TRAIN moving north along the tracks, and Holly's wish would be granted. Not one for sitting still, she concentrated on her reflection in the window glass. Dark trees streamed past and provided the necessary contrast to observe her fair skin. She checked her pink lipstick, tugged her ponytail tight, and straightened the loops of her blue hair bow. She fluffed her long blonde curls hanging over her shoulder just as the landscape shifted from forest to farmland, and she could no longer see herself in the glass.

The train began a long turn through a shallow valley. A rhythmic bouncing caused Holly's stomach to bobble towards her chest, and the passengers in the cabin to stir. This was her opportunity to share a new glance with the man sitting across the aisle from her. From her place facing forward on the train, and his facing towards the rear, it was hard not to catch his eyes. As it was, the last hour and a half had gone by far too slowly and looking at the man was the only thing entertaining her.

His dark brown hair, long but pulled back into a small knot, and his obviously tailored and pressed white collared shirt had held her imagination for longer than it would have under less boring circumstances.

She knew his sort; likely an associate at some high-power law firm but funded by his daddy's money. She wasn't passing judgment, of course. Growing up the daughter of a successful banker and the prettiest Kentucky debutante, meant that Holly knew her way around the upper crust of the up-state crowd. But this man, sitting near enough for her to catch the amber scent of his Chanel Bleu cologne, with his perfect posture and overly groomed facial hair, was juxtaposed by his man-bun and worn-in canvas messenger bag. His appearance offered her curious mind more questions than answers. But now, an introduction would be awkward after a dozen reciprocated smiles and without so much as a greeting passing between them.

"You're staring," the smooth masculine voice said and tore her from her contemplation.

Shaking her head at having been caught, she rolled her lips between her teeth. "I'm so sorry. I really wasn't meaning to stare at you," she said, though there was no law against people-watching.

So much for needing a bump in the tracks to allow her to interact with him when she could have just said 'hello'. She did the next best thing to avoid further embarrassment and hid her eyes behind her hand until she was sure he'd lost interest. Despite her attempt to disappear, warm fingers gently peeled her self-made mask from her face. As light hit her lids, Holly peeked out of one cracked-open eye.

Parted lips and rounded cheeks framed a thin line of white teeth. "Hi," he said, leaning across the walkway.

Opening her eyes fully and replacing the bewildered tension wrinkling her expression lines with a smile that matched his, she repeated his greeting. "Hi. I really wasn't staring. I was just looking in that general direction and kind of, I don't know, spaced out for a minute."

"You don't need to explain. I'm a very captivating man."

"Aren't you confident?"

He grinned. "Theodor, and I like to think I'm charming." He extended his hand from where he sat alone in a group of conversation seats.

"Holly. Nice to meet you," she said and reached her hand out in response. His fingers slid around her palm and cradled hers. She could feel him temper his strength as he relaxed his grip and released her. "I really am—"

"Don't you dare try to apologize again," he said and settled back into his chair. "You were checking out my hair, huh?"

She swallowed down a giggle that she was sure was a taste of self-consciousness. "To be honest, kind of. I've been sitting here trying to figure you out."

"Do I need figuring out?"

Wasn't that the million-dollar question for anyone in their mid-twenties? Holly had been in a string of unproductive jobs and unsuccessful relationships since college, which had been a waste of her time. What she needed to figure out was how could a humanities degree help her with what she really wanted; to open an ice creamery inspired by the gardens of Monet. She should have gone to culinary school, or business school, but no, she had chosen a field of study for the singular purpose of studying abroad on her parents' dime. Perhaps it was she who required figuring out, not Theodor. She shook her head. "I was only wondering where you're heading."

"I'm visiting a friend in Christmas Cove. Do you know it?"

She bit her lip thinking she might have cause to run into this man again. "Yes, actually. I'm from Elizabethtown, right next door." *Small world*, she thought because the train had several more stops on its way.

"Small world, huh?" he said with friendly eyes.

"That's what I was just thinking." This time, a giggle did

escape her throat. She didn't know what to say next, and too much time had passed with them glancing at each other.

Theodor let out a strained sound of amusement and turned to gaze out his window. She supposed that was that; her insecurities ruining yet another promising interaction. Even with his head turned from her, she was helpless to peel her eyes away from him.

"You're staring again," he said and caught her gaze in the window's reflection.

"I was watching the trees outside. Did you see the horses back there?" She saved herself with a white lie.

"Really? Horses?" he said with skepticism painted on his face.

"Yep," she said with a head nod. "Lots of horses. Maybe you blinked and missed them because the train's going so fast. You should really work on your watching skills."

"I'll do that. Thanks for the advice," he said and returned to his view through the glass.

"Sure thing." She wanted to die. "I'm usually better at this, I promise."

He turned in his blue upholstered seat and faced her. His knees almost reached to her own, and he leaned in. "My name is Theodor Black. I'm from New York. My parents hate my life choices, and I'm running away to Christmas Cove to make a life for myself where no one knows me. I'm twenty-seven years old. Single. Good-looking, obviously, and I'm usually better at this too." With his info-dump, he returned to his side of the aisle and fixed his eyes on the empty set of seats in front of him.

Single? She was single after finding that snake, Rinaldi, in a compromising position with another woman last year. Since then, she hadn't been searching for a man to keep her company at all. But Theodor's brown eyes and confident grin told a story she was dying to know more about. Getting up from her chair, she swung a leg over his and flopped into the vacant seat beside him.

"What are you doing?" he said with smile lines crinkling

above his cheeks that told her he was entertaining her bold move instead of being irritated by her switching seats.

"You don't mind, do you?" His answer came in the form of stunned silence. "I'll take that as a no. Now, tell me, Teddy. Can I call you that? What do you do in New York?"

"Nothing, now." His brows pinched together, and his eyes shifted towards the ceiling as though the words he wanted might be plastered there. "I'm in between jobs right now. That's why I'm heading to Christmas Cove. My friend, Alfonso, works as a chef at a local resort and he asked me to come help with a culinary night for some of the guests."

"So, you're a chef? Is that what you did back home?"

"Not as much as I would have liked. If my father had it his way, I'd be paying my dues at an Upper Eastside law firm or sitting sidecar at a high-profile trial," he said and unknowingly confirmed her earlier suspicions.

"You're a lawyer then?"

"If by lawyer, you mean I've passed the bar? Then yes."

"So why aren't you practicing law, seems like an okay job if you ask me," Holly said.

"Well, I didn't think so," he said with an edge that she was sure wasn't directed toward her. "Sorry. It's just a sore subject."

Disappointing parents was something she was well versed in too. Although, in her father's eyes, Holly could do no wrong, she knew it bothered him that her ambitions in life had taken her down a more unconventional path. Her mother on the other hand would only be satisfied at the sight of Holly walking down the church aisle towards a man with a hefty trust fund and an even more prominent pedigree.

"Navigating parental expectations can be hard, especially when every single choice is debated over like you're a pawn in their game," Holly said and crossed her legs towards him, closing the distance between their knees.

"You speak like you know me," Theodor said.

"Sorry."

"Don't be. I like it. Most of the people I spend time with are more than happy to play their part, but you sound like you have experience with that too."

She nodded and bit her lips between her teeth. "My father is a banker, and my mother is basically a spoiled Southern belle who wants me to be like her. I'm just not. No matter how I try to be what she wants me to be ..." Holly paused and considered what blow-back she would get next time she saw her mother. She could only avoid her for so long, now that she was moving back home. "Let's talk about something else."

"Do you like puffins?" he said without skipping a beat.

His question had her brain scrambling to change gears. Despite her request for a new topic, puffins was quite an unexpected one. "I guess so."

"No. Nope. You cannot sit on both sides of the fence on this question." He chuckled at himself, which sort of annoyed her that he was enjoying this round so much. "In my experience, I can tell a lot about a person based on how they answer this question. So, think carefully."

"I suppose I've never given it much thought. They're those little black and white penguins, with the parrot beak, right?"

"Wrong." His hands flew to his face, and he pulled the skin down his cheeks under the weight of his finger and exposed his wide eyes. "They're not related to penguins at all. Not even close. They're not even cousins."

Holly could tell he was teasing her, and she supposed she could just as easily trip him up with questions about horses if she really wanted to turn things around. The straightforward thing would be to give him an answer, and he clearly wanted her to be as enthusiastic about the bird as he was. But Blake Holly Hollis doesn't play nicely like that. Blake Holly Hollis is a winner.

"Alright. I've made up my mind." He was on the edge of his seat, and at some point, had cupped her hands in his. "I do not like puffins. They look ridiculous and, did you know, they're not even related to penguins like they should be?"

"Hey! I just told you that." He removed his hands from hers and threw them in the air in disbelief.

"Someone had to call it like it is." Retrieving her phone from her dress pocket, she pulled up a photo of a puffin on her browser and turned the screen towards his eyes. "They're kind of silly looking, like clowns. Don't you think?"

He chuckled in his throat. "They're disgusting little things, and I hate clowns."

"Then I passed your test?" Holly said and stashed her phone.

Still jovial, Theodor nodded his head. "I can't trust someone who likes puffins, is all."

"Are you one of those birders who travel around cataloging every bird you meet? How do you know so much about puffins anyway?"

"NGK."

"Sorry, I'm not following," she said and shook her head trying to place the acronym.

"National Geographic Kids. My Granny bought me a subscription when I was little. I suppose I can blame her for my adventurous side. I remember opening that first issue and seeing a world that was so unlike the concrete playground of Manhattan, I knew I needed to get out eventually and explore it all."

His reasons for leaving the city might be different than hers, but it seemed like they were both running away from the versions of themselves that everyone else wanted them to be. She knew that her life would never feel like her own unless she blazed her own path. She wasn't stupid though; she wanted her father's blessing—and money—to do it with.

"So, you had the world at your fingertips, and you chose to go to Christmas Cove?" she asked, wondering why a man as good looking as Theodor would want to live somewhere so obscure.

"Yep."

Holly appreciated how sure of himself he was. "It's a pretty great place. I won't lie. But small. Like it's absolutely tiny compared to Manhattan. And I don't think you're ready for it. Everyone will know your business before you do," she said with a giggle.

"That shouldn't prove to be an issue. Apparently, I'm totally fine spilling my guts to strangers."

"We're not strangers, are we? I'm Holly. You're Teddy. We've shared more looks during this train ride that I think I have in my past three relationships combined, and we both think puffins are weird little clowns. I'd say that's a good start to a wonderful friendship."

The train brakes let out a sharp cry as they engaged with the steel tracks. Elizabethtown Station was announced over the loudspeaker. The dense green trees outside the window ceased being a blur to the point that now she could make out individual branches and leaves. "How long will you be in town for? Maybe we can bump into each other sometime."

"I'll be staying for a while. And I think I can find time to bump into you again soon."

The train came to an unceremonious stop and the doors slid open up ahead of their seats. The cabin hadn't been full and emptied quickly. Holly took her brown-leather Louis Vuitton travel bag from the overhead and threw it across her shoulder. Behind her, Theodor waited patiently for her to move up the aisle.

"You want help with that?" he asked.

Holly suspected his offer was out of politeness and not because she looked incapable. "That's okay. Thank you though."

As she walked towards the door ahead of him, her energy stretched out from her body in hopes of touching his a little longer. Their conversation had been brief, but full of life. Consumed by attraction, she wanted to know more about this man from Manhattan and was desperate to run into him while he was in town. She gave him a final glance over her shoulder before jumping down to the concrete platform, just beyond the painted yellow line, and turned around. "Do you want to—"

Theodor mimicked her jump and landed with his toes only inches from hers. "Come to the Chocolate festival with me tonight?"

"Yes," she said without delay.

"It's at the Foundry. Do you know it?" he asked and walked backwards towards a man waving him over from the front seat of an old red pickup truck.

She nodded, of course she knew the Foundry. It was the hottest new place in the area. Joining in on the Cove's revitalization was one of the reasons she was moving back home in the first place.

"Eight-thirty." Theodor smiled and switched his focus to the man in the truck. Teddy hopped into the front passenger seat and greeted the driver with a spirited embrace.

Beyond the red pickup, Holly spotted a sight for sore eyes. Holly waved at Millie, her childhood best friend, who was walking up to the station from the parking lot. With her other hand, Holly caught the ruffled hem of her skirt just as a breeze attempted to expose her.

CHAPTER 2

THEODOR BUCKLED HIS SEATBELT ACROSS HIS LAP AS ALFONSO drove away from the station. He twisted in his seat and peered through the dirty rear window of the cab at the most beautiful woman he had ever seen. Her long, robin's egg-blue dress seemed to float on the breeze as she perked up on her toes, waving to another woman walking from the parking lot. Even from this distance, Holly's smile was wide enough to shine in the morning sun.

"Alfonso, I think I'm in love," Theodor said and let the sight of her diminish as they traveled around the street corner. Returning forward, Theodor patted his hands on his knees and let out a shallow breath knowing there was much to do before seeing Holly again later. "How are you?"

"*Buono*. Good. But bro," Alfonso said in his Italian accent and tsked his tongue against the roof of his mouth. "The ride was short, no? And you're in love?"

"I don't know, there's something about her. We spent most of the trip trading smiles. I was sitting there hoping for a reason to talk to her, and when I finally did, I made an absolute fool out of myself. I word-vomited and told her things I never say to anyone."

"What is this word, word-vomit?"

"It's like when you tell someone way more than you should. Once you start talking, you can't stop."

"Ah, *si. chiaccchierone.*"

Theodor would look that one up later. He knew enough of Alfonso's native language to make it by in conversation, but not much more. French, on the other hand, was something they both knew equally poorly, with the majority of their common words being culinary related. Broken English or not, it was still the best way for them to communicate.

"I can't wait to get back into a kitchen. You'll need to get me up to speed for the festival events tonight because ..." he looked out the front windshield. "I invited the woman."

Alfonso clapped his hands together, and Theodor reached over and held the steering wheel true. "Who taught you how to drive, bro?"

"Teach Alfonso? Dominic Toretto."

"You learned how to drive from watching a movie?" Theodor shook his head. "Of course you did."

"Vroom, vroom motha-fu—"

"Just put your hands back on the wheel, will you?"

Alfonso kept his focus forward for the duration, which Theodor appreciated. Today was not a good day to die, not when he had a date. *A Date? Is that what it was?* Holly had said yes to him with zero hesitation. Now, heat rose behind his ears, and he rolled down the window for some fresh air.

The ride to the Foundry followed a lonely country road along tree-lined fields and stone walls. The black, asphalt pavement cut a clean line around each hillside and traveled along a crest with a panoramic view. This wasn't his first time in town, but the lush summer foliage made the scenery appear much changed.

Theodor had visited Alfonso in the spring and had fallen in love with the small town. He wasted no time planning a move there. Christmas Cove had felt like home from the moment he stepped foot on the cobblestone main street and dipped his toes in the ice-cold shoreline of the little lake.

Liking the small town was made easier knowing his best friend, Alfonso, was there. The Italian transplant had become the head chef at the Foundry, a high-end retreat where city dwellers could come and get a taste of the outdoors while staying in luxury accommodations. The first time he stayed in town, he'd crashed on Alfonso's sofa. This time, he had booked a cabin at the Foundry until his place in town was ready to move into.

They parked in an empty spot at the rear of a blackened barn structure that served as the resort's main gathering space. Harbour House, as it was called, contained the dining room, a relaxing gathering space in front of a two-story stone fireplace and hearth that would give a medieval castle a run for its money.

Inside, they walked from the service door past a storage area and a very well-equipped gym. He sucked in his stomach at seeing the line of Peloton bikes along one wall, and the sound of his mother's voice echoed in his mind. *How can you expect to take care of a spouse if you can't take care of yourself?* She always thought he was out of shape.

Theodor's excuse was chocolate. He was in as good physical condition as he'd been in years, but it was true that while juggling law school, culinary school and working all hours at the Champagne Bar at the Plaza, little time remained for other lifestyle improvements. Working out was easier when he had no one or nothing else taking up his precious time.

Perhaps this change—this place—would be everything he needed to start a new life for himself.

"This way," Alfonso said and led them to the *Cucina*, the resort's dining facility.

"You know I was here a couple months ago, right?" Theodor reminded him as they pushed through the saloon-style kitchen doors. "When I helped with that insane wedding cake?"

"Alfonso no think you could do it," he laughed.

"I admit, I'd never made chocolate look like a coral reef, but it was a beauty when I was finished with all the pieces." The cake, as challenging as it was to create, had made a huge impact on his decision to give up all of his parents' dreams for him and follow his calling to be a chocolatier. "Now show me what ingredients you were able to source for me for tonight."

Alfonso bent down and pulled out a large blue tub, about three feet across and two feet deep, from underneath a long stainless steel work surface. The way he grunted while lifting it, Theodor expected it to be full of rocks. Peering inside, it might as well have been stones. Stacks of raw chocolate bars wrapped in clear cellophane filled the container, and it was no wonder Alfonso had a difficult time lifting it.

"Enough chocolate, no?"

Theodor washed his hands and began unpacking the goods. He organized the bricks into piles on the worktable and began sorting out his recipes in his mind. "How many people are coming?"

"*Cento.*"

"Really, a hundred guests?" he repeated to make certain, and Alfonso nodded with a silly grin. "I suppose I'd better get to work. You had better get to making dinner too."

Alfonso nodded and headed into the walk-in cooler at the far end of the kitchen while Theodor placed the last of his items on the table. It was apparent that he was underprepared for the event, even though he'd relayed a list of all his supplies to Alfonso, he just hadn't done a big event like tonight's before.

There was no time to second guess himself now. A stream of about ten guests flowed through the kitchen door and approached his spot at the center of the space. With smiles all around and eager, wide eyes taking in the stacks of ingredients, he supposed he was meant to do something with them.

"We're here for our chocolate demonstration," one of the women said as she hugged close to a tall man.

He put up one finger indicating that they wait a moment. "Alfonso?" he said and chased his friend into the cooler. "What are those people expecting me to do?"

Alfonso poked his head out of the long plastic curtain pieces and drew his head back inside. "Oh. They pay extra for teaching about chocolate."

"Is that all? You could have mentioned it before now."

Alfonso shrugged and shoved Theodor back out into the open kitchen space. A white jacket slid up his arms from behind and Alfonso patted him between his shoulder blades. While walking to the guests, Theodor buttoned his chef coat and smoothed the front.

"Tell me, who knows anything about chocolate?" he said and came up with a fast plan to provide an experience they would not soon forget.

The guests were easy to please and seemed happy to learn how to melt chocolate properly. They filled moulds with the creamy mixture and snacked on some fruit, drizzled with the mouth-watering remnants. The afternoon passed quickly, and the satisfied guests departed the kitchen.

Alfonso spent his afternoon tossing pots and pans around. His cooking style was chaotic and messy compared to Theodor's. Theodor took the time, even in its smallest measure, to clean as he went along. Chocolate was a feisty enough ingredient to work with and required a care and attention to detail that Theodor's brain was well suited to handle. He liked things to be orderly. Clean. Predictable.

In the thread of desiring precision, a career in law was an obvious choice, but so was his love for the chemistry and art of chocolate. He took his time and prepared the dozens of truffles, bars, and morsels for the festival, while Alfonso worked on the dinner offerings. Each dish included chocolate as a featured ingredient.

"I'm here to help," Grant, the resort's manager, said as he walked into the kitchen. "What can I do?"

Theodor bumped elbows with the man, as his hands were busy working a silicon mould off what he hoped would be a big hit with the guests: a rose shaped truffle. "Nice to see you again," Theodor said.

"I was not surprised when our Alfonso gave me the news that you planned to make the Cove your new home. And I can't tell you how excited we, here at the Foundry, are to be working with you again," Grant said.

"I'm glad to be out of the city, that's for sure." He sucked in a deep breath of fresh air. "I appreciate the help, but I'm actually just waiting for these to set-up properly before arranging them all," Theodor said as he finished the batch in his hands. "Actually, I think I'll get cleaned up in the meantime. I still smell like train, you know?"

"Why don't I show you to your cabin," Grant said.

Theodor removed his white coat and hung it on a hook beside the door before throwing his small bag over his shoulder. "I'll be back in a little, Alfonso," he shouted into the kitchen. Alfonso's arm protruded through the door-flaps of the walk-in cooler and waved him off.

"How's the weather been up here this spring?" Theodore asked Grant as they walked out the front door.

"Much dryer than last year," Grant chuckled, "but we've had enough rain to keep the lake looking good. It should be a fun summer with all the water sports and activities we can do."

It had been ages since Theodor had been in any body of water other than a pool. Looking past the wide lawn and scattered cabins, the afternoon sun illuminated each tiny ripple and wave on the lake's surface, and he hoped he could find time to take a dip. "Which one's mine?"

Grant pointed to the square lodge nearest to the short dock and patted Theodor's shoulder with his other hand.

Theodor took a step from the concrete pad outside the Harbour House doors to the gravel path and was snatched back. A golf cart screamed around from the far side of the building and the driver pulled it up right where Theodor's foot had landed only a second earlier. The older man, with white hair, tidy and combed behind his ears, and a warm smile shifted to park and came around to Grant with his hand extended.

"Thanks for bringing this around," Grant said. "I have some things to check on up the hill after I drop Theodor at his cabin."

"I could have just walked, you know?" Theodor said and shook the old man's rough hands.

"Pa. It's nice to meet you," the man said. "I've never met a real chocolatier before. My wife, Carol, can't wait for your shop to open."

Theodore was surprised he had a fan already. "How do you know—"

"Small town. Everyone knows everything about everyone," Grant said and hopped in the front seat while laughing. "Now let's go."

Theodor nodded at Pa and joined Grant in the golf cart, ready to finally get cleaned up for the evening and ready to see the woman from the train again.

CHAPTER 3

Sitting in Millie's passenger seat, Holly fluffed the chiffon layers of her skirt. After the train ride, she needed a shower and a new outfit. She had changed out of her blue, floral, day dress and slipped into a shorter, pink frock for the evening. Opening the visor mirror, she checked her lipstick and straightened the bow at the crown of her head.

"Are you sure this isn't too much?" she asked her friend.

"Holly ..." Millie pulled the car around the Foundry's circular drive and parked in front of the large barn doors before answering. She took Holly by her shoulders. "You are spectacular, as always. Plus, you have nothing to worry about. This is just the Foundry, not the Ritz."

"It's not the location I'm worried about."

"Whoever this Teddy is, I'm sure he's wonderful. Alfonso mentioned he was picking up a guest chef from Elizabethtown today. If Alfonso likes him, I'm certain he's a good man."

"That's also not what I'm worried about," Holly said and, in her mind, played back her interaction with Teddy. He had seemed so into her, and even touched her hands most unexpectedly. "Just tell me one thing."

"I heard someone bought that empty storefront across the street from you," Millie said.

Holly shook the confusion from her thoughts. "What?"

"You told me to tell you one thing. That's my one thing."

"Do you think this is smart for me to jump into something right now? It's only been a few months since I broke things off with Rinaldi," Holly fluffed her lashes in the rearview mirror.

Millie caught Holly's gaze. "I think you're overthinking this. It's just chocolate, which I'm thrilled to try. Look at it this way. You enjoyed your time with him, and you like him. Does it matter if you're romantic or just friends?"

Holly had to admit that Millie wasn't wrong. Everyone can always use another friend. Why not Teddy? "You're right. That actually takes a lot of pressure off. Should I lose the bow?"

"Leave it. Your hair looks great pulled back like that."

Holly got out of the car and walked towards the resort's glass-front doors. Candlelight spilled from inside and illuminated the gravel walkway with a warm glow. As they approached the door, a sweetness floated out into the evening air. She breathed in and savored the delicious scent as she entered the grand lobby.

Dozens of guests gathered in little groups around cocktail tables. High above her, an enormous crystal chandelier—with more bulbs than she could count—sprinkled dim light around the space. Holly took in the sights but only as a side effect of looking for Teddy.

"You good?" Millie asked. "I'm going to find Alfonso."

"Is there something going on between you two that I should know about?" Holly bumped hips with Millie.

"I'll let you know when or if there's something to tell." Millie winked and slinked away.

When Holly finally spotted Teddy laughing with a group on the far side of the room, she fought the urge to run. It would have been too late anyway, as his gaze fixed on her. He stilled. His eyes widened and his mouth parted as he took her in and nodded to his right.

They each walked towards a towering stone fireplace flanked by two-story windows, never taking their eyes off each other. She was sure she held her breath the entire time, until they met in front of a velvet settee. His mouth parted and his eyes smiled, the way she had witnessed earlier, like he was about to say something. Silent pauses made her self-conscious. Before she could make a small-talk remark, he broke the tension.

"Wow. You look ... wonderful," he said, while amber specks flashed in his brown eyes.

A blush heated her cheeks, and she twirled around. He might as well get a good look at the whole ensemble that she stressed over picking out. "The event looks like a success. All these people." Holly scanned the room, partly because his gaze was intense and partly to see if there was anyone present who she recognized.

He leaned in near the side of her face. "Don't worry about running into anyone you might know here. Most of these people are guests of the Foundry, not locals."

She turned towards the sound of his voice and found herself brushing noses with the man. He smelled earthy and sweet and tangy all at the same time. No doubt his aroma was laced with the various flavors and ingredients he had worked with to pull together for the chocolate festival. She licked her lips at the thought and watched him mimic her movement.

Why was this man so enticing? It couldn't only be the fact that he was basically dripping with cocoa. Except that he had been just as intriguing on the train ride and had no hint of confectionery on his person at the time.

Needing distance, she stepped back. Right over the back of her stiletto and fell down onto the sofa. She wanted to die, but Teddy plopped right beside her to cover for her. "Thank you."

He grinned. "I have something for you. Wait here?" Teddy got right back up and disappeared for only a moment before returning. He carried with him a round wooden tray with a glass dome covering an arrangement of sweets. He placed the dish on the coffee table and removed the dome.

Unable to contain her excitement at the sight of so many pretty chocolates, she clapped, and a little squeal escaped her mouth. "You made all these? They look incredible."

"This is what my father thinks I'm wasting my time with." Teddy took one of the deep brown squares and held it up. Little gold flakes glittered in the candlelight. "May I?"

Holly closed her eyes and parted her mouth. The cool chocolate brushed her lower lip, and she took the morsel with her tongue. It took little time for the chocolate to begin to melt into a rich smooth texture and she opened her eyes. He raised his brows in anticipation of her analysis. All she could offer was a grin and nod of approval until she could swallow it down.

He took another, lighter-brown piece and handed it to her this time. "Bite into this one."

She removed a thin paper wrapper from the bottom and sunk her teeth into the outer layer. The thin outer shell cracked easily, and a mandarin liqueur spilled across her tongue. The acid opened the pores in her mouth and the flavor seemed to multiply. Overwhelmed and intoxicated, she nearly forgot she was surrounded by people.

Her unease must have been showing when she covered her mouth with her fingers until she was done enjoying the treat. He didn't seem to mind. If anything, her reaction seemed to thrill him. Like a scientist making a discovery or a magician fooling a crowd, Teddy's smile turned from a smirk to a wide grin. He bit his lower lip the way people do when they try to disguise their true emotions.

"Good, huh?"

"Has your father actually tried any of your work? I mean ..." she shook her head as the last flavor settled into her mouth.

"You really like it?"

"Teddy, I don't know what kind of lawyer you were going to be, but I guarantee, you'll never get a reaction like this from any judge or client." Holly reached for another chocolate. "Which one next?"

Teddy pointed to a green one in the shape of a small daisy. "That's a new one I'm trying out tonight. Let me know your honest opinion."

She paused.

"What's the matter?" he asked.

"Nothing, just, no one ever asks for what I think. I'm told what to think or say. Especially when I'm at a social event like this." Holly looked around the room and realized this was one of the first times she had attended a function, save for college parties, where her mother or father weren't lurking nearby.

"I know what you mean," Teddy said. "You don't need to worry about censoring yourself around me. I have enough of that from everyone else in my life."

She nodded. "I like that, Theodor Black. Same rule applies to you." Holly placed the green chocolate on her tongue and waited for the flavors to warm and reveal themselves to her tastebuds. "Mint? No. wait." She let the entire thing melt and knew it wasn't mint, but something akin to it. "I give up. What is that stunning flavor?"

"Indian cardamom. It has hints of ginger and lemon." He took one for himself. His eyes closed as he savored the flavor. "I just can't decide if I love it or hate it."

"Love it," Holly said without hesitation.

Teddy stood and motioned with a head tilt for her to follow. He could have offered her a hand, but moved away before she could ask. She slap-dashed in her high heels to catch up with him, while he easily weaved his way through the thinning crowd. He danced around a serving table and absconded with two champagne glasses out the main doors.

Another guest passing through the same door, held it open for her. The warm night air kissed her skin, and a soft breeze played with the fluffy layers of her skirt as she pranced across the driveway. Waiting for her, debonair in his black three-piece suit, Teddy leaned his back against a stone pillar. The top buttons of his white shirt were left undone, and his smirk should have warned her to turn around before she made yet another poor relationship judgment.

He handed her a flute, clinked the rim of his glass on hers, and she knew it was too late. The bubbles fizzled and rose to the surface of the liquid like the butterflies in her stomach trying to escape.

"Walk with me?" Teddy asked, though they were already moving away from the party.

The bubbles became indistinguishable in her glass as they walked down a gentle sloping sidewalk away from the building's light source. Small solar lanterns lined the path leading down to a wooden dock, but barely cut through the dark night. The distance wasn't far, and they filled the air with their small talk about the weather, and the sweet song of the cricket choir. At the end of the dock, Teddy turned and sat on a wooden railing. Instead of drinking his libation, he drank her in.

He looked at her as though he was seeing so much more than just a pretty face. Ignoring the pleasant sensation building in her gut, she held her glass up and rested her bum on the same railing next to him. "To following your dreams." Their glasses rang in harmony.

"And to new friends," he said and took a drink.

Friends? The way he had taken her in as she twirled in her dress or the way he placed the chocolate in her open mouth felt like more than just friends. She pondered any deeper meaning to his words while hundreds of bubbles danced in her mouth with her next sip. He wanted honesty, so maybe she should ask him the question she'd been pondering all day.

But Blake Holly Hollis wasn't known for being patient. "Can I ask you something?" He nodded and sipped his bubbly. "When was the last time you had a girlfriend?" *Slick*, she thought. She wanted to know just how available he was before dedicating too much energy to something that might not work out.

"I told you I was single," he said and smirked as though he knew she was fishing for something. "But that's not what you're after."

"Am I that transparent?"

"Yeah. But I like it," Teddy said and downed the remnants of his champagne. He placed the glass on the square post holding up the railing and took her glass, stashing it with the other.

Heat climbed her neck as Teddy moved closer to her. The warm night air didn't help things. She wiggled and created a little bit of a breeze under her skirt which elicited a reaction from him.

Teddy raised his brows and deep lines cut across his forehead.

"What? It's hot out here. This is what girls do." She swished her hips and the pink ruffles on her skirt swayed back and forth.

Teddy moved his hips like hers and mimed tucking his hair behind his ear. "Like this?"

Holly smacked his chest. "Stop teasing me."

"I like teasing you." He captured her hand against his torso and held it there. His breath was shallow, and his palm clammed up in seconds.

"Do I make you nervous?" Holly said and closed the small distance between them, looking up into his brown eyes.

Teddy nodded and his Adam's apple bobbed up and down as he swallowed.

"Why?" Holly asked. Her head tilted to one side making it easier to see his expressions.

"For starters ..." he took her hand over her head and spun her around. Her skirt flew out, making a wide circle. He stilled her once she faced him again. "You're beautiful."

She knew she was egging him on by batting her lashes. "And? I'm sure you've had your share of pretty women."

"What makes you think that?"

"A charming, good-looking guy with your family background? You probably have your pick of any number of socialites," Holly said and let go of his hand.

"You think I'm good-looking?" Teddy said. "Charming too?"

Holly nodded and felt flatfooted in this conversation. It was her turn to swallow down the nerves. "You're pushing your luck."

Teddy hopped down and closed the distance between them. "And what if I wanted to kiss you right now? Would that be pushing my luck?" he backed her against the railing. Her hands caught the top piece of wood behind her bottom, and she arched her back away from him. She wasn't afraid of his advance. She wanted it. She craved the thrill of his attention. His arms hemmed her in, and she was at his mercy.

"Tell me, Holly, what do you really want to know?" he spoke into the tender tissue near her ear. His breath warmed her skin, but the air matched the temperature just as fast. The sensation was unsatisfying, and she wanted more.

She leaned her face against his. The short, groomed hair on his cheeks and jaw pressed into her flesh and lured her into wanting to find the smoothness of his lips. "I want you to kiss me," she whispered. The closer he moved to her mouth, the higher her heart rate climbed. Butterflies flitted inside her belly but transformed into red flags at the memory of her past relationships. She slid her fingers in between their mouths just in time.

Teddy cleared his throat and backed away.

"I need to know if you really like me, or if I'm just another flighty socialite to add to your conquests," Holly said, but her query had a sharpness she hadn't intended. Her question had sounded more like a character accusation than an invitation for honesty. "Teddy."

He backed off and tucked his hands into his black pants pockets. "Even if I did like you, I get the feeling you would have a hard time believing it. Am I over the target?"

"You might be." She was surprised by how clearly he saw her.

"Do you trust me?" Teddy said with a one-sided grin.

Holly liked the idea of trusting him but wasn't quite there yet. "I think so. I want to."

Teddy turned to walk back to the resort, and she grabbed his elbow, knowing she had ruined the moment. "Well, Holly, I suppose I'll have to help you make up your mind. In the meantime, why don't I walk you back up?"

"I'm sorry, Teddy. I didn't mean to offend you. I've just been hurt—"

He stopped and put a finger on her lips. "I told you to stop apologizing. We all have stuff in our pasts that messes us up. As for my conquests, as you call them, I have none."

His declaration was hard to believe. A guy as good looking, charismatic, and well-mannered as Teddy had no notches in his belt? She was sure there was more to his story now and was determined to get the whole tale. "Will I see you again soon?"

"I'm staying here at the Foundry for the rest of the summer, maybe I'll bump into you again." Teddy walked her towards her car where Millie and the man who had greeted Teddy at the station, Alfonso, were sitting on the hood engaged in conversation. Slowing, Teddy spoke in a hushed tone. "I'm not offended." He stopped and held her hands, standing face to face. "I'm glad you came here tonight."

"Me too." She thought he might kiss her now. His eyes trained on hers, and his tongue darted out and wet his lips. She stood taller and tucked his hands around her waist, but a hoot—coming not from a nearby owl watching the show, but from the couple sitting on the car—broke their connection. Another moment ruined. At least this one wasn't her fault.

Teddy released her and met up with the man. "Alfonso." Teddy placed an arm around Alfonso's neck and removed him from the hood of the car. "We have a mess to clean up, no?" he said the last part in a pseudo-Italian accent which caused the chef to laugh as they walked towards the building.

Millie hopped down. "What was that all about?"

Holly watched the men go inside. Teddy stopped and nodded before disappearing on the other side of the door. "I think I'm in love."

"Okay, TayTay. Let's pull the reins on this one and get you home. You have a big day tomorrow at your shop."

CHAPTER 4

THE AMBIENT MORNING LIGHT MADE THE VACANT STOREFRONT windows into an ideal mirror. Holly checked her reflection and straightened her white hair ribbon looped around the base of her ponytail. Leaning in, she pressed the puffiness from her under-eyes, thinking she looked more drained than she felt. She had stayed up later than she should have, going over her business plans and concocting reasons to accidentally bump into Teddy again. Her scheming would have to wait because today, she had no time to be tired. Today, she had a shop to build.

"Holly," Millie yelled and waved from where she was parked down the street. She jogged, with her brunette, swingy, bob-style haircut bouncing around her jawline, and caught up with Holly. "Didn't sleep much last night?"

"Is it that obvious?" Holly shook her head and flexed the muscles in her cheeks in an effort to look as sprightly as she felt. "I don't know why, but I stayed awake thinking about getting my new sign today, and about … Teddy Black."

Millie put an arm over Holly's shoulders and hugged her in. "You've got it bad."

"Do you know he was going to kiss me last night." She slapped a hand against her forehead. "And I can't believe I almost let him."

"Maybe he was just teasing you?" Millie guessed.

"Yeah. And whatever he was doing, I liked it." Holly threw her hands up and stepped up to the edge of the curb. In her white and blue espadrilles, she teetered like she was falling from a cliff, not a six-inch step down. "If he kissed me or not. Being with him was … thrilling. But I'll worry about him later. I have bigger things to think about right now. Like that." She presented her hands towards the large sign being hoisted out of a wooden crate across the street.

A man sitting in the cab of a small crane had hold of the custom placard and was lifting it up towards another man positioned on a cherry picker at the front of her new store. Holly clapped her hands together and made her way to the middle of the street. Seeing her shop's name plastered in pretty letters made her dreams seem real. In that instant, she went from a girl with an idea to a badass businesswoman.

The man in the cherry picker motioned for Holly to move closer. "Just make sure it looks right before we secure this thing," he said.

The crane operator lifted the sign up over the sides of the crate and let it rest ever so slightly on the sidewalk. Holly smoothed her fingers along the neon script and said the words out loud. "Cups & Cones Creamery. It's really happening, isn't it?"

"I'm so proud of you," Millie said.

"This has to work. There's no way I'm moving home with people who want to see me fail."

"Just your mother," Millie added, and wasn't wrong.

Holly nodded to the man in the cherry picker for him to continue the installation. Behind her, a flurry of activity began across the street where earlier she had checked herself in the window reflection. Two pickup trucks pulled up alongside the curb and blocked her view, but her curiosity as to what could possibly be interrupting her big moment could wait. She returned her focus to the installation at hand.

The crane lifted the green and white striped placard with pink neon lettering up to the space between the top of the double doors and the second-floor windows. The soft shades popped in front of the white-painted bricks and black-framed windows. The arch over the front door had been the feature that had sold her on leasing this particular building. The other vacant space, the one across the street, lacked the old-world charm that she was looking for to house her ice cream shop.

"If Francesca Bridgerton had a shop, this is what it would look like," Millie said. "I'm excited to get to work on the build-out."

"I'm so glad you went to design school. I have an eye for what looks good, but I've never had the knack for putting it all together," Holly explained. "That's why I dress the way I do every day. It just makes things easier when I have a closet full of pretty dresses and matching bows. It's one piece of clothing to put on but it looks like I spend way more time getting ready than I actually do."

"I admire that," Millie said and pointed to her jeans and white linen button down. "Why do you think I have a closet full of outfits just like this. It's like a uniform in a way."

"Better than black turtlenecks like Steve Jobs used to wear,"

"You're far more stylish than Jobs." Millie giggled.

"Now, if I can be half as successful!"

Millie pointed up to the sign being fastened into place. "This is a start!"

The man on the cherry picker yelled down for Holly to confirm the positioning before attaching the remaining bolts. Millie moved into the street and blocked traffic. She signaled to

Holly when it was safe for her to stand in the road and have a good look.

Glad tears began to well in Holly's eyes before she took it all in. She stepped backwards over the uneven cobblestones, reassured in her choice of shoes, and held her hand over her brows like a visor. The sign looked even better from her vantage point in the middle of the roadway, which meant that passing vehicles or pedestrians on the other side of the street would easily be able to see Cups & Cones while coming or going down Main Street.

"A little higher on the right side." She motioned to the man in the cherry picker. "Other right," she yelled and waved her hand.

As she waited to approve the adjustment, a nearby truck honked its horn wanting to be let through. Millie held up a finger to the lady in the front seat, while Holly stepped back for a view of the full scene.

"That's it, boys!" someone behind her yelled out. *Another opinion never hurts*, she thought, as her rear end collided with something. She spun to see what she had run into and glimpsed a man doing the same turn-around.

"I beg your pardon," the man said as he caught her gaze. "Are you alright?" he asked, and she knew from his voice who it was.

"Teddy? What are you doing here?" Holly said with a smile that hurt her cheeks.

"Me? What are you doing here?" His smile stretched with the delight at seeing her. "I'm leasing this empty store over here. I'm opening that chocolaterie that I mentioned."

Holly looked past his body at the vacant space that she had just been using as a makeshift mirror and was now abuzz with activity. No less than a dozen workers had arrived on site and busied themselves at demolishing whatever character had remained in the building. She supposed, after having checked out the same place and rejected it, that the best way to renew it was to start from scratch too. "But I thought you were just here for the summer."

"I'm staying at the Foundry for the summer, or at least until the second floor of this building is ready for me to move into."

He's moving here? This was a development she hadn't expected. Was she happy about it? "You're opening a shop too?" She wanted to clap from the joy of knowing she would definitely be bumping into him again while suppressing the rising vomit in her gut for realizing she now had a direct competitor for the still-growing customer base in town. When Christmas Cove was incorporated into Elizabethtown a year earlier, the beleaguered main street screamed for revitalization. It was the main reason she had selected the Cove for her shop in the first place, which begged the question: What was his reason?

As though he read her mind, he said, "I visited a few months ago, and I've been working ever since on getting this project off the ground."

The woman inside the waiting car honked her horn again. Teddy drew Holly to his side of the street, while Millie darted back the other way.

Millie waved her arms above her head. "I have to get to work. You okay?" she yelled past the few cars that had been waiting for them to move from the street, and Holly nodded. "The sign looks great! I'm really excited for you." Millie ran down the sidewalk towards a pink Victorian house where she was working on a renovation.

"Your sign?" Teddy asked and shielded the sun from his eyes as he read the words hanging above her door. "Cups & Cones Creamery? Is that yours?"

"I told you I was opening an ice cream place." She could feel the tension grow as the realization dawned on him. "Well, this is it. So, I guess we're going to be neighbors."

"Competitors," he said under his breath, though she heard him just fine. His brows pinched. "I knew someone had leased that place. To be honest, it was my first choice, but someone snagged it before I could secure my funding. But I thought the name on the lease was Blake. Do you know him?"

Holly raised her hand like she was answering a pop quiz question. "That's me, I'm afraid." She put her hand out to shake his. "Blake Holly Hollis. Nice to meet you."

Teddy shook her hand with the speed of a sloth as he processed the information. "Blake?" He paused. "If I had to lose the bid to someone, I suppose I'm glad it's someone as nice as you are."

His response was magnanimous, the way a properly raised man should behave. "I guess I'm happy that we'll be seeing more of each other. When are you planning on opening?"

"As soon as possible. The challenge is finding workers around here," he said.

"I know, it's a nightmare with all the construction going on, the labor force hasn't really caught up to the need."

It was no secret anymore that Christmas Cove was having a resurgence. Not long ago, Christmas Cove was the most happening place to visit. But when the lake had dried up, so did the businesses. It was happenstance that Elizabethtown had incorporated the small town and helped the place recover at the same time Holly began looking to spread her wings.

Peering down at Teddy's white sneakers, it was clear she wasn't alone in her desire to get in on the action. It was clear that more people than ever were looking to cash in on the town's popularity all year round. It was the same reason Holly had chosen the location. Growing up in the area, she knew the Cove was the perfect place for her to open her creamery.

"I'm aiming to be open by the Fourth of July," she said.

"That's soon. Cross your fingers," he said and held his fingers up to her. "And I'll cross mine."

Holly was happy for Teddy to be her business neighbor. Regardless of their budding romantic connection, having a friend across the street from her could be a big advantage, she could use to leverage her success. She held up her crossed fingers to him. "We'll both need some luck," she said as someone walked by and slipped a flyer into her hand. "What's this?"

Teddy took the paper and read it out loud. "Attention all small business owners. The Elizabethtown Chamber of Commerce in conjunction with a local anonymous benefactor, is awarding a one-time grant totaling fifty-thousand dollars. Open to all shops on Main Street. Must apply no later than June twentieth. Winner will be announced on Independence Day."

Holly clapped her hands together and bounced on her toes. "A grant? That's exciting! Are you going to apply?"

"Of course I will," Teddy said with a smile. "I could use the money."

"I don't *need* it, but I'm a winner," she boasted. "Consider it already in the bag."

Teddy folded the paper and slid it into his jeans pocket. He leaned into her ear. "I wouldn't be so sure."

"Is that a challenge?" Holly did not want a challenge, not from the man who she liked. She had lied about not needing the money, but she would never admit it. Her father had informed her only days ago that her mother was threatening to cut her off again. Her mother's support always had strings attached, and even though Holly's father wanted to help financially, Holly knew he would eventually capitulate to whatever her mother wished. Right now, her mother wanted Holly to join her in raising horses. The longer Holly held out and blazed her own way in life, the tighter her mother pulled the strings.

"I'd like to see you try and beat me," Teddy said. His side-cocked grin and bright eyes let her know he was engaging in playful banter.

"Don't underestimate my ability to make you regret those words," she taunted back.

"I'm more motivated—"

"How do you know my motivation level?" she said, though he talked right past her.

"—than you are to make my shop a success. And I happen to be the most organized person you'll likely ever meet. I can plan my way through any circumstance." Teddy's confidence was showing, and she liked it.

"It's fifty-thousand dollars. That's life changing money for a small business. Do you know what I could do with all that?" she said as her imagination sparked with new ideas in her mind. "I could really use it."

"Well, if we're both vying for the award, we could make this a little more fun. I propose a wager."

The suggestion of raising the stakes interested her. "Are you sure you want to gamble against me? I wouldn't underestimate my ability to win at all costs." Holly flicked her long mane over her shoulder and aimed to walk away.

Teddy captured her by the hand and wrenched her back to him. She collided with his body and his arms held her against him. "You're scared?" she teased.

"Of you?" he chuckled low in his throat. "Never."

"I don't think it's a good idea." She squirmed in his arms but not enough to get away. "But if I did, what bet do you propose?"

"If I win, you have to carry my products in your shop for the first month, and if you win, I have to—"

She cut his thought short. "You'll have to go on a proper date with me, wherever I choose." What should have sounded like a playful threat, came out more like an invitation. Holly didn't think these stakes were that bad, "Deal?"

He nodded. "Shake on it?" He let her go and put his hand out.

"I have a better idea." She pushed his hand aside. "Kiss on it instead?"

He smiled at her suggestion and closed his eyes. Taking his jawline in her hand, she perked up on her tiptoes and brushed her nose against his. His chest rose and he held his breath. The tension in his muscles told her he was waiting for her lips to be on his. But he would have to wait for something as sweet as that.

Holly pressed her mouth against his cheek in the fastest peck she had ever given. Before he knew what hit him, she had darted across the road between passing cars and turned to face him from the other side of the street. "You're gonna lose, Teddy!"

CHAPTER 5

Arriving on Main Street the next morning, Holly parked her dad's silver Tesla Roadster down the street from her shop. She left plenty of room for work vehicles to have easy access to her space, she also parked close enough to the local coffee house to pick up some treats. With two coffees in hand, she headed straight for Teddy's place and hoped he was there so she wouldn't be responsible for downing two double shot espressos by herself.

She peeked her head inside the open front door. "Teddy? Are you in here?" After waiting a whole two seconds for a response and hearing only the sound of a drill, she let herself in and followed the noise to its source. "Teddy?" she said coming around the backside of a long wooden countertop where she found him crouched down.

Startled by her touch on his shoulder, he spun towards her with the electric drill pointed at her like a weapon. He removed his fogged-up safety glasses and huffed. "Don't you look just like Tim the Toolman."

"Who?" she asked and looked down at her clothing. She had thrown on her most work-appropriate outfit, a pair of denim shorts and pale pink floral crop top. The tool belt was more for dramatic effect, but the caramel-colored leather hanging from her waist topped off the outfit and made her look way cooler than she was. "It's just regular me, here with a gift for you." Holly held out the steaming paper cup for him. "Cappuccino with extra foam."

Teddy stood and sniffed the rising steam. "Poison?"

"No." She handed it over. "I just thought you might need some energy today. With all this work you need to get done. I mean look at his place. You think you'll be open in a month?"

"Are you trying to get in my head, Blake Holly Hollis?"

The way he said her name, like a dirty word, left her speechless. She closed her bedeviled, gaping mouth and hid behind the rim of her cup. *Was he trying to get in her head?* She would not allow this man to toy with her, especially when so much was on the line. "I'm just being a good neighbor. Where are all of your workers anyway?" She scanned the mostly empty space that had been teaming with men in hardhats yesterday.

"The demo crew finished up a day early, so it's just me today," Teddy said and sipped his drink. "Anyway, I figured I could get a head start on some of the lingering layout questions. Like this bar." He ran a hand along the long edge of the old bar-top. "I was planning on tossing this thing, but I think it's worth saving. Just look at this mahogany."

"What are you going to do with it?" She was genuinely curious what use he could find for a bar. "I would have just thrown it out or used it for firewood."

"Somehow, I doubt Blake Holly Hollis has ever made a fire."

She certainly had not, but he didn't need to know that fires and outdoorsy things weren't really her vibe. However, she would make an exception for frolicking through a beautifully manicured garden somewhere. "Are you going to call me by my whole name from now on?"

"So long as you call me Teddy, I'll call you whatever name I want."

"If that's how you're going to be, I won't stop you." In truth, she liked the way her name flicked off his tongue like a delicacy. She met him beside the bar and ran her fingers along the wooden top until she touched his. "So, Teddy, what are you going to do with the firewood?"

Teddy put his coffee down and regained use of both hands. He motioned towards the ceiling and dropped his gaze in a straight line down towards his feet. "A ladder."

"Ooh. How exciting," she teased.

"See, if I turn it upright and attach some sliding wheels, I can use it to go along this whole back wall. I want to use my supplies as décor in the upper shelves."

It was actually an interesting idea, she had to admit, and so nostalgic. It was a shame she hadn't thought of something similar for her own shop, though her interior design style was more Victorian garden and less Charlie and the Chocolate Factory. "It's a nice idea, Teddy, really. Teddy," she said, adding his name again just to irritate him. She had no intention to cease using the pet-name because she enjoyed hearing him call her by hers too much. She hid a giggle.

"Thank you, and thanks for the joe." He tapped his cup against hers like a salute to their growing relationship. "I really should get back to work though, if you don't mind."

"Do you want any help? I wore my worker outfit," Holly said and did a little shimmy.

"I see that. You look just like all the other guys." Teddy approached her. "It's the tool beltbelt for me."

"You like it?"

He nodded with a smirk that pulled up on one side. His teeth showed between relaxed lips and nearly made her wish she *had* kissed his unshaven face yesterday.

The peck on the cheek was meant to aggravate him, but it had the unintended effect of frustrating her too. He looked like a man that could kiss well, she considered the fullness of his lips and the pillowy smooth texture that she was sure would be like silk against her skin. Heat climbed her neck, and she backed away from him.

"I should go. You know where to find me if you need help with anything."

"I thought we were working against each other to win that fifty-k?"

"Who say's we're not?" Holly knew she was teasing him and patted the steel head of a shiny new hammer hanging from her hip. Her intention to distract him had dramatically backfired. She would be thinking about him the rest of the day, not the other way around.

CHAPTER 6

THEODOR HADN'T SEEN ANY MORE OF BLAKE HOLLY HOLLIS following her unannounced coffee delivery yesterday, though he'd peered across the street more times than he wanted to admit in the hope of glimpsing her bouncy walk or flippy ponytail. As innocent as she seemed, he had a feeling that he was in for more than just a friendly, yet distracting, visit. He hungered to experience more of their playful, back and forth interactions.

Currently, his stomach growled from smelling the warm bread and spiced meats from the stack of sandwiches he was carrying in his arms. "Definitely the sandwiches," he said to himself as he made his way inside his shop. "Alright boys. Break time. I got lun …" The space was empty. Not a soul was in sight. He had been gone for only a half hour while running over to the Foundry and collecting the food order from Alfonso.

Various tools lay on the floor or were situated on a temporary folding table. One of the workers had left their phone on the windowsill, still blasting music into the echoey space. The eerie scene caused him to wonder if the rapture had happened and he alone was stuck on this side of Armageddon.

Just to make sure he wasn't losing his mind, Theodor

checked the small yard at the rear of the building, thinking perhaps his workers had gone out back for a break. The long overlooked and unkempt outdoor space was begging to be used again, and he hoped that he would have funds left over to spruce it up. Better yet, he could win the money. Wishful thinking for the future aside, the yard was deserted, just like the rest of the shop.

While in the quiet spot, a low chuckle emanated from somewhere nearby and definitely outdoors. Theodor jogged back through the front and searched the streetside for the culprit. When he heard the sound again, he ran across the road—dodging a car that honestly was going too fast for a downtown street—stumbled up the curb, and through the creamery front door. He walked right into the center of a circle of men. His men. His workers sat on folding chairs arranged in a large arc, laughing and eating.

"Hey boss," one of the men said while gnashing a piece of pizza in his half open mouth. "We're on break."

"I see that." Theodor looked around for Holly, likely prancing around in one of her cute outfits. "What are you doing over here? You guys know I brought you fresh lunch." He took a slice from a man's hand and tossed it back in the open box on the floor. "Better than this crap."

"This crap is the best pizza in the county," Holly's voice rang out from behind him.

He turned on his heel. She stood in the doorway. Her blonde hair fell in soft curls around her shoulders, not in her typical ponytail, and her yellow dress floated in the breeze moving up the street and through the open doors. She was a breath of fresh air, and she took his away.

He choked on his first word and began again. "Best pizza? Says who?" As he spoke, he moved to assist her with the four two-liter bottles of pop spilling out from her arms. Why was he helping her when he should be cross with her for luring his workers away? He didn't know, but he knew aiding her was the right thing to do. "Here, let me get those."

"A gentleman." She smirked and handed over three of the bottles. "Now ..." She took a slice of pizza in her free hand and held it up to Theodor's face. "Try it before you say something else ridiculous."

He was left with no choice. He took a bite and cut the strings of cheese with a fast yank of his neck. The yeasty crust, not too thin and not too thick, complimented the sweet and tangy tomato sauce, and the creamy cheese and blend of herbs mellowed all the flavors together. He licked his lips. "Fine, it's good."

He hated to confess, but it was no wonder his workers had found their way over to her shop if this was the bait. She pushed the pizza between his open lips, forcing him to take ownership of the whole slice. Growing up in Manhattan, arguably the pizza capital of the world, he had tried his share of pies, but this one was exceptional, just like she had proclaimed it to be.

He followed her like a little puppy dog past the circle of men to an ornate, brass table with a piece of plywood placed on top where a glass slab likely once laid. He arranged the pop and unpacked the sleeves of red disposable cups.

Holly lifted a small cooler to the table and flipped open the lid. "I figured we can help each other."

"I appreciate the thought, I do, but I already bought sandwiches for my guys. You could have coordinated with me."

She placed a hand on his forearm, a soft delicate hand. "I'm sorry. I don't want to cause problems for you. I'll pay you back for the sandwiches, or we can have them for an afternoon snack." She scooped a cup into the ice. "Can I get you a drink?"

His mouth was watering for the ice alone. She had sprung for the delicious little nugget ice, and he thought he felt himself falling in love with her right then. As she poured the soda, he looked around at her mess. Almost no demo had been completed.

A dozen paint cans lined the base of a wall littered with paint swatches. Unopened boxes of chandeliers were stacked in a corner beside an arched doorway. In another area, she had piles of bags overflowing with flowers and greenery.

Beneath the mess, he really did like the overall charm of the space, and he was still sad his bid had been too low.

"Scoping out the competition?" Holly said and stole his attention back by positioning her face in the foreground of his vision. "I'm just messing with you. This place is a total wreck right now."

Her giggle was the sweetest tune to ever tickle his ears. But was she really just innocently messing with him or were her actions working to undermine his ability to win the grant? She handed him a filled cup, and he brought the cool fizzing liquid to his lips. "Poison?" he said, only half kidding.

Holly cocked her head to one side and smirked, but a fire behind her brown eyes was a warning. She was playful, sure, but he sensed a devious streak in her too. "You got me all figured out," she admitted. "Here you are scoping out the competition, and here I am trying to off mine." She motioned a cutthroat at him, and he knew he was in for a fun contest to win that money.

Before he could retort, she took a tray, loaded up with ice cold drinks and walked towards the workers—his workers—and handed the cups out. A sly side eye and a grin like the Grinch was all it took to make him go from wanting to be her friend, to knowing that, for the time being, they were rivals. Everything she was doing was to throw him off, distract him, get under his skin, and win.

So be it. Once the grant was awarded in a few weeks, he could work to uncoil all the layers of Blake Holly Hollis. Her desire to win meant that she was playing against him whether he participated or not. It was time for him to put up more of a fight.

He pointed at her smug face. "You are slick. You know that? Here I thought we were helping each other, but you're playing a little dirty," he growled out and helped his workers to their feet. He piled pizza boxes in the hands of one dumbfounded man and retrieved the tray of drinks from Holly. "Time to go. Come on, you lot. We've had just enough hospitality for the day."

"You've never seen dirty. I told you I was motivated." Holly pantomimed fist-fighting with him.

"Didn't you strike first?" He shifted his eyes to the remnants of the lunch scheme, empty paper plates and cups, a half-eaten cheese pizza, and his workers scurrying back across the street. "And, if I had to guess, your little coffee stunt yesterday was really round one." He had her pegged.

Her slack-jaw and pinched brows let him know that she knew he was right.

"Toodeloo," Theodor said and waved his fingers over his shoulder as he exited.

CHAPTER 7

THE LATE AFTERNOON SUN POURED IN THE FRONT WINDOWS OF Holly's store. She had picked this place because of the abundant light inside the south facing frontage. With all the light, came about a half hour where the sun shone straight inside and all the way to the back of the shop, which is why she could only see the silhouette of a man standing in her doorway.

Whoever the person was, was too short to be Teddy. She had managed to get through what remained of the day without so much as a glimpse of him and shook off the guilty feeling she'd been carrying around since courting his workers with delicious pizza.

"Parcel for Blake Hollis?" the man asked.

"That's me, thanks. You can leave the package on the windowsill. Do I need to sign for it?"

He placed the medium-sized box where she indicated and scanned the barcode. "Good to go, ma'am."

He left, and she shook off the icky way she felt whenever someone called her *ma'am*. Growing up, her mother demanded Holly use polite southern manners. No matter how often she heard the word directed at her, it never sounded quite right. She always had the urge to look over her shoulder, half expecting to see her mother standing there, arms crossed, and shaking her head at the utter disappointment Holly had become.

Holly put down the paint brush and covered it with a damp paper towel. She had every intention of coming back later to finish the wall-mural she was working on. Right now, she had other, more pressing things to handle. The delivery held her next offensive blow.

"Knock. Knock," Millie said from the doorway.

Holly pulled the stack of papers from the box and held them up. "Look what I got!"

Millie took the top paper, a flyer advertising the new creamery with a perforated section along the bottom that featured a half-off coupon. "It looks good. But I can't say the same for the way things are looking in here. Will you be ready in time?"

"I'll do whatever it takes to make this place a success. You know that I'm afraid this is my last chance at making my own way. My parents are tiring of my 'whimsy'," she said and motioned air quotes. "If this doesn't work out, I'll be out all my savings, and probably have to go work with my mother at the stables."

Millie threw her arms around Holly's shoulders. "It won't come to that. We're going to make this work. Tell me how I can help."

"Right now, you can help me pass out these flyers." Holly handed her friend a roll of painter's tape.

Millie held it up. "Really? Where on earth did you find ballet-pink painter's tape?" she laughed and slid the roll over her wrist.

"I have connections."

"With whom? Amazon?"

Holly shrugged, but of course, she ordered it online like a normal person who needs a stash of pink painter's tape. "Let's get going."

Holly left the shop doors open to air out the mural she had been working on and repositioned the flyers in her arm. "Left, or right?" She looked both ways at Main Street. The sun was just about to go down and the street was coming alive. Even though the area was only newly coming into a revitalization, it was teeming with activity. On both ends, new shops and restaurants had opened and they drew people to the area.

On weekends, the square in front of the old City Hall building was a gathering place. Even now, live music echoed down the cobblestones as the band warmed up. Soon, the whole square would be filled with families and out-of-towners out enjoying the night air. Across the square, a restaurant had a lovely outdoor seating area with fairy lights strung over a brick patio. Little bistro tables served double duty for eating and enjoying the music.

Folks were trickling into the area, but it wasn't quite time to hit the crowd yet. Holly looked the other direction where a few customers were busy coming and going from the Cove Boutique, a quaint little place that sold everything from fresh flowers to girly dresses and featured many local artisans. The shop was one of her favorite places to hunt for unique items, and it rivaled any big-city boutique: a slice of the city in the quaint little Cove.

She looked straight out at the soon-to-be chocolaterie, seemingly closed up for the weekend. All the workers had scattered, and no lights were turned on. "I have a better idea," Holly said and stepped out into the road with Millie close behind. "Tape me."

Millie tore a section of tape, several inches long, and handed it over Holly's shoulder. "Are we really doing this?"

Holly answered with action when she plastered one of her eye-catching flyers to Teddy's door. She stood back. The pinky-floral background and bright-green lettering screamed for the attention of any passersby. "I like it there."

"You're asking for it," Millie said and clapped her approval.

"And I obviously support you, one-hundred percent." She handed over another stretch of tape.

Holly and Millie worked as a team, sticking dozens of flyers to every light post, bench back, and empty window along the street. Holly forced a flyer into the hands of anyone walking by too.

"We're opening in a few weeks, make sure to come by for a scoop with your coupon," Millie said as she handed out the last flyer. "What now?"

Standing away from the main crowd that had gathered by the fountain. Holly's hips swayed to the rhythm of the bluegrass music. "Reminds me of my mother." She smiled thinking about how easy things were before her mother's horses started winning big races. Holly had spent her childhood in the stables, that's how she had met Millie. "Do you remember all the trouble we use to get into when we were little?"

Millie laughed before answering. "I remember doing things we *should* have been in trouble for, but we almost always got away with it."

"Come on, you think they didn't know that two little girls were sneaking around, switching equipment, or letting the horses into the wrong pasture? They had to have known it was us, and they let us have our fun anyway," Holly said and giggled.

"Do you remember when we fed your mom's favorite horse the edible glitter?"

Holly covered her mouth with the back of her hand. "I will never get that sight out of my mind. There was sparkly poo everywhere."

"Your poor mom, she cleaned out the stable that day because she was embarrassed for anyone else to have to do it. And she never said a word to us about it."

"When she used to be nice." Holly lamented. "But that's what I'm saying. They had to know who was causing mischief. And I'm not sad for a second that we had a childhood as good as that."

Reminiscing about the fun they used to have, gave her an idea that she hoped she wouldn't regret. "You want to get into some trouble tonight? Like old times."

"No, but also, yes!" Millie whispered with excitement all over her face.

Holly turned to go back to the shop, the music fading behind her.

Millie scurried to keep up. "I know that look. What are we about to do?"

Holly turned at the entrance into her shop. "Close that door behind you, will ya?" She headed for the table where all the fresh supplies were arranged and retrieved two painter's suits. She tossed an unopened package to Millie and unpacked one for herself. The white jumpsuit was huge. She held up the material that easily could accommodate someone twice her size, but it was all she had.

As Millie put her suit on, without question, Holly searched through a box of spray paint, and caulking. "It's in here somewhere," she said, and Millie appeared beside her.

"What are we getting?"

"I'm looking for the chalk spray. For windows. It looks like this," she held up a can of bright blue spray chalk that she had used a few days ago to lay out the floor plan. "I want the gold one or yellow, or white."

"Why do you have these?"

"I got them for my front windows. It's like paint, but it's easier to wash off. So, I can change the display in the windows. But right now …"

"We're spraying Teddy's windows, aren't we?"

Holly nodded and captured her lower lip between her teeth. "Keep looking. I want to get this done while everyone is down at the fountain."

Millie began taking the contents out of the box and lined up the cans and tubes on the table making it easier to see what they were. "Isn't this vandalism? I don't want you to get in real trouble."

"It's only chalk. Harmless." Holly followed Millie's example and set aside any of the cans of spray chalk. The only light in the space came from the streetlamp outside and the twinkle-lights that hung between both sides of the road.

Once they separated the products, Holly took her phone from her pocket and shone the torch on the display. "Look for the gold one," she whispered though they were alone. "Wait, here's one, but you need one too."

"Oh, no. I'm not going to jail for you," Millie said and backed off. "I'm only staying to make sure you don't get arrested."

"Fine," Holly said and started shaking the container. "You can be my lookout."

"You're gonna shine like a spotlight in that," Millie said. "Here." She handed a can of dark paint to Holly. "Spray me."

Holly began shaking the can but handed it back to Millie. "I have a better idea." Holly walked to the long wall and peeled plastic wrap off a large can of paint. She took the roller in her hands and proceeded to paint her front side. Unable to reach her back, she passed the roller to Millie.

"This is quicker," Millie said and pressed the roller up and down Holly's backside. "Now do me."

Holly repeated the process on her friend until she was certain enough that they no longer appeared like bright rays in the dark. While unsuccessfully holding in giggles, the two headed out across the street as though they were taking part in a spy caper. Hunched over and bent low, they made their way to Teddy's storefront unseen, though possibly heard as their nonstop snickering and shushing reverberated off the brick façades and cobblestone street.

"I can't believe you're going to ruin his window."

"Hush up, Millie. I'm not ruining anything. I'm just fixing it." She felt impulsive and light like she had indulged in one too many glasses of champagne, but she was totally sober. Holly supposed the feeling was from the exhilaration and danger of possibly being caught doing something questionably legal. She looked at Teddy's window display that read, *Coming Soon, Up State Chocolaterie.*

"Coming never, more like it," Millie said with a snort.

Holly snapped her fingers. "That's it." She shook the can again and rotated the nozzle for a fine spray line. "Make sure I'm all clear."

"Got it, Picasso. Do your thing."

Holly was grateful to have such a good friend, and happier to have her partner in crime back in her life after they had gone separate ways to college. It was humorous they had both said they would never move back to town, and here they both were, making a life and career in the place where they had started.

With the can held as high as she could reach to the store's window, a vehicle's headlights lit her up as it turned onto Main Street. They both dodged the light and tucked themselves behind one side of the bay window where it met the front door. Plastered against the wall, holding their breaths, Holly and Millie exchanged looks until the car had passed by.

"I thought you were on lookout," Holly teased. "That was too close."

"Just do what you're going to do, and do it quicker."

Holly shook the can one last time, and, with a plan in her mind, went right to work. She sprayed the gold paint over the existing words and changed the word *soon,* to *never,* in the prettiest cursive lettering she could form with the spray nozzle. Her writing matched the old-world charm Teddy had mentioned he was aiming to capture. With the job nearly done, she stood back to look.

"Are you finished? There's someone walking this way."

The words didn't look quite right and were missing some flair. "Almost done." Holly walked confidently to the window and began to spray the gold chalk paint in smooth, pretty lettering when her phone rang. *Back in Black* screamed from her phone and filled the entire atmosphere. She dropped the can and dug inside the long-zippered section of her suit for her device. "Shit. It's Teddy."

Millie joined Holly's side and they both fumbled for the phone, trying desperately to answer the call or silence it. "Answer it already!" she whispered and finally hit the green button to accept the call.

Holly stood up straight and took a little breath to calm her voice. "Hello, Theodor. What's up?" she said, smacking her forehead when she realized she had called him by his proper name and not his pet name. Her voice had that fake-calm sound that she had perfected while attending events with her mother over the years.

Her words probably had all the hairs on his neck standing on end. There was an elongated pause and Millie motioned to her, asking what was going on.

Holly flapped her hand at Millie. "Are you there?" she said into the receiver.

"I was calling because I thought we could talk. I was thinking about how we both want to win that money, and how you said we could help each other. I don't like being on opposing sides …" he said.

She looked up at her half-finished handiwork, and her thrill was replaced by a twisting guilt in her gut. She motioned to Millie to walk across the road, and they began to move, crouched down like sleuths. "I don't know why you think there's anything to work out. We are just two small business owners vying for the same thing. If it's not the money now, it'll be the customers later. I don't really see how we could do anything for one another."

"So, you're saying we'll never be anything more than two people who own shops across from each other on Main Street?" Teddy said.

"Do you really think I would help out my competition?" she said and knew it wasn't true. "I just mean—"

"Save it," Teddy said with an all too justified sharpness. "Where is the charming, puffin-hating girl I met on the train? Tell me one thing. If there's nothing between us, why did you answer my call, and why are you sneaking away from my place right now?"

She paused and looked up. The man walking down the sidewalk towards them held up a phone and waved the lit-up rectangular screen at her. Understanding the man to be Teddy, she hung up and ran.

CHAPTER 8

THEODOR WAS UNABLE TO RECALL A TIME DURING HIS LIFE WHEN he'd felt so bewildered. Blake Holly Hollis had not been kidding when she warned him about going up against her. What he thought was a friendly competition seemed like much more to her. What he couldn't wrap his head around was why a rich girl like her needed the extra money in the first place. Perhaps her reasons weren't unlike his own. At some point, a person must make their own way in life.

He was determined to learn the truth of her motivations, one way or another. For now, he would let her have her fun at his expense. The competition would end eventually, and he hoped no matter what the outcome would be that he would land in place beside her, not against her.

Theodor thought about her blonde hair as she had fled from her criminal activity last night, her long curls and romantic ribbon swinging in the breeze created by her impressive speed. Instead of using his fingers to comb through her glossy locks, he was scraping and scrubbing chalk graffiti from his front window. He had to give it to her, her little stunt had brought his shop a lot of attention and many onlookers.

He smiled down at a small child who was licking a hard candy lollypop. "You like sweets?"

The little boy with a round face nodded and grinned behind his confection.

Theodor leaned down while holding the top handle of his step ladder. "Do you like chocolate?" His question elicited an even wider grin from the child and an enthusiastic up and down head nod. "Come back and see me when my store opens, ok?"

The boy's mother took his little sticky hand, and they walked away.

Back to work, Theodor took care in removing the gold script lettering Holly had sprayed atop his original window art, trying to salvage what he could. Most of the chalk paint had come clean with soap and water. He used a small flat edge razor blade and flaked off what remained of the tiny spray particles, careful to avoid the real lettering underneath. He was just glad she hadn't used real paint, though it covered his *Coming Soon* sign all the same.

"*Buongiorno*, bro," Alfonso said as he approached from down the sidewalk.

Theodor stepped down to the ground. "I wish it was a good morning." He pointed with his thumb at the remnants of the golden graffiti. "This was Holly and your friend Millie."

"No! Millie is not bad woman," Alfonso said and waved both hands in disbelief.

"Maybe not, but she was here last night, all the same." Theodor took advantage of having stepped away from the window to see what else he had to do to finish the removal. The glittery gold paint that remained caught the morning light and shone against the luscious wood interior. "I'll need to thank Holly for this idea. I'm about to order my permanent decals and now I know what color and font to go with," he said only partly joking. "The gold actually looks great."

"*Si.*" Alfonso grabbed onto Theodor's shoulders and jiggled him. "Give Alfonso job, yes?"

Theodor looked across the street at Holly's quiet job-site and wondered what mischief she was out planning at that moment. Though he hoped at some point they could put this little rivalry away, the reality was beginning to crystallize: Blake Holly Hollis was trouble, and she had ensnared his imagination. She was equal parts a woman needing to be loved and one who needed to be put in her place.

Theodor had little time to outdo her one-sided game and turned his attention back to Alfonso. "What's going on with you and Millie, anyway? I saw the way you were looking at her the other night after the chocolate festival." Theodore asked and gathered his ladder.

Alfonso grabbed the bucket and tools and held the door open. "*Vite.*"

"Vite? Grapevine?" Theodor let the question linger as he placed the ladder just inside the door.

"Millie ... how you say?" Alfonso used his pointer finger and gestured a curling motion. "Wrapped around Alfonso's heart."

Theodor understood. "She's like the tendril on the vine. Alfonso, you're such a romantic. I like her, I do, I just hope she can keep Holly from doing something stupid again."

Alfonso smiled with his hands on his hips. "We work?"

Theodor clapped his hands together. "Today's goal is to get the kitchen set up. All my beans are coming in two days' time, and I have to get roasting or I won't have any chocolate to sell on opening day."

Theodor explained where the display cases would be positioned. He planned on having three distinct counters where he could feature differing themes. At the front, he planned for a small bistro-style eating area where guests could enjoy their selections, and if his liquor license came through in time, he would pair a variety of wines with his chocolate flavors.

Alfonso nodded his approval along with several grunts and they walked into the back space. Theodor motioned around the space, prepared to explain the work that still needed to be completed, but there was nothing to explain because there was nothing in there at all. "Where's all my equipment?" His hands covered the sides of his head, and he wanted to rip out his hair. All he could think was there had been far more shenanigans last night than some shoddy graffiti on the front window.

"Did you lose or ... move it?" Alfonso said and opened the rear door to the back patio.

"I think I'd remember moving it," he said, and wondered, for a split second, if Blake Holly Hollis had anything to do with his missing kitchen.

"Look here."

Theodor made his way out back. A shade structure stood over a section of patio with all of his equipment lined up and organized. Doubtful that Holly had cleaned out the space and arranged the heavy items, he walked back into the front of the shop and saw a note written on the whiteboard. His construction manager had left the note explaining where everything was and that the floors were still wet last night.

The entire reason he had been out last evening was because the old wood floors were being cleaned and resealed. In his annoyance, he had forgotten all about the work being done. And now, he felt guilty at having mentally accused Holly of being so wily.

Theodor took the hand-truck and made for the patio. Now that his kitchen was ready to be outfitted, he wasted no time at getting things going. Once the earthy scent of roasting beans was permeating the air down Main Street, he would feel like he was on the fast track to opening day.

He and Alfonso made quick work of moving the roasters, counters, sink station, and drying racks inside. There was one wall where the roasters had to go, the electrician had supplied the correct power, and a system was put in place to vent outside. The remaining modular items could be configured to suit his needs, but right now, he needed maximum roasting and drying space.

Using the hand truck, and brute strength, they positioned the counters in an 'L' shape to make the roasting process faster. Later, Theodor would need to focus on stocking his confections. Like always, he had a plan and would stick to it.

He stood back at the entrance of the shiny kitchen. Excitement coursed through his veins. "I think this might actually work, Alfonso." The space was organized and had a good flow from one workstation to the next. Other than needing a good wipe-down, he could see his dream coming together.

Alfonso threw an arm over Theodor's shoulder and looked on with him.

"I appreciate your help today."

"No problem, bro."

The front doorbell jingled and caused their work to stop. "It's probably one of the laborers."

"Hello in there." The feminine voice was not one of Theodor's workers. "Alfonso? Are you here?"

The grin on Alfonso's face stretched wide and returned to neutral just as fast as it had appeared. "Millie," he said with a blush evident on his cheeks. His grin returned and Alfonso slapped Theodor on his back as he made for the front.

Curiosity caused Theodor's feet to follow his giddy friend. "You like her a lot!" he whispered from behind, and Alfonso replied with a sharp shush.

Spotting her target, Millie embraced Alfonso with a smile plastered across her face. As happy as she seemed to see the chef, her light demeanor dissolved when her gaze met Theodor's. "I'm so sorry—"

"Save it. I know what you did," Theodor said, interrupting. "You have a lot of nerve showing up here today."

"Despite what you might think, I can't actually control her, you know. Plus, it was only chalk," Millie said, "I didn't come here to fight. I actually came for him."

"You can let Holly know that her plan backfired," Theodor said and crossed his arms for effect. "I've had more interest today than ever."

"I guess, you're welcome," Millie said with a cock of her head.

Theodor stayed quiet, not wanting her to know how Holly had burrowed under his skin. He would deal with Holly when the time was right. Alfonso could deal with Millie, though by the looks of his friend's goo-goo eyes, Alfonso was a lost cause.

Alfonso put his hands out like he was asking permission to take Millie out. "Time to go."

Irritation tensed in Theodor's neck. "Millie, before you go, can you tell me why she's fighting dirty to get the grant money?"

Millie shrugged. "Holly's a winner. If she sets her mind to something, she'll stop at nothing to get it." She stepped just outside the front door and paused to add, "If you can't beat her, join her. Although my advice is to stay out of her way."

"Do me a favor, Millie. Tell your accomplice that I need to speak with her."

"We're getting drinks later. I'll tell her."

Alfonso shrugged on his way out.

"Traitor," Theodor shouted only half kidding.

Across the street, he saw a striking blonde skip into the creamery as though she had not a care in the world. Theodor had never known a person without any cares. In his experience, the people with the most to lose often pretended to care the least. Sure, he could go to war against her and retaliate tenfold, but his gut told him that there was more to her story to learn.

CHAPTER 9

THE LAST THING HOLLY WANTED TO DO WAS RUN INTO TEDDY after being caught gold-handed outside his storefront. There was no way he wasn't mad at her for the chalk stunt, and she did not enjoy feeling guilty that she had had some fun at his expense—even though they were embroiled in a competition. Holly spent the day justifying her actions in her mind and staying away from Main Street until she had to go in. At some point, she needed to work on her wall mural before getting drinks with Millie and some of her friends.

She had wrongly assumed her visit would go unnoticed, but Teddy had been standing in his doorway when she skipped down the sidewalk. Upon seeing her, he dumped a bucket of dirty water down the street drain and retreated inside his shop. Thank goodness their interaction had been nearly non-existent. She could get her painting done and get to a much more enjoyable event. Girls' night was just the thing to get her mind off Teddy Black.

. . .

HOLLY HUGGED A CHILLED WINE BOTTLE AND THREADED THE STEMS of three more empty glasses between her fingers. She had been in the middle of telling her story to the other women when the rosé had run out. Holly had offered to get more supplies from the kitchen while their hostess, America, greeted a few late arrivals to the party.

"Holly," America said and waved her over. "I want you to meet some of my friends from the Cove. This is Jenny, Thandie, and this is my beautiful mother, Vivian."

"It's a pleasure." Holly took America's mom's hands. "You own the boutique on Main, right?"

"That's right. Call me Vi, please."

"I love your store. It's become one of my favorite places to shop for goodies and girly dresses." Holly's excitement was evident in her wide smile and rapid speech. She felt a bit like a fangirl and twirled around, showing off her newest purchase: a pretty green frock with delicate chiffon ruffles that cascaded from the hips to her calf.

"It suits you perfectly," Vi said.

"Thanks. I can't wait for my business to open in a couple weeks." Patience wasn't ever her strong suit, but what's to be expected from a girl who was given everything her heart desired as a child. Patience and planning were personal skills she needed to improve on if she were going to succeed as a business owner, and shooting to win the grant money was providing the focus she desperately needed and motivate her through the home-stretch.

"Alfonso tells me that your creamery is coming along well," a tall woman with dark hair said. "I'm Thandie. I work with Alfonso. That guy can't keep anything to himself." She sniggered and motioned to take the glasses from Holly's hands. "Let me help you."

"I know what you mean. But I don't know who's worse, Alfonso, or Millie," Holly said and handed over the stemware.

As they moved away from the front door, Jenny, America's

other friend who had come in with the others, took Holly by the arm as though they were old friends. "I must prepare you ..." she paused her low tone. A hundred things ran through Holly's mind at what could be so dangerous as to necessitate a warning from a stranger. Jenny snatched the bottle from the crook of Holly's elbow. "I hope we have more where this came from." Jenny laughed and walked ahead of a stunned and amused Holly into the parlor.

"I'll get another," America said, having overheard Jenny's remark. She patted Holly on the shoulder as she passed by and made her way to the kitchen at the back of the house. "Jenny talks a big game, but one glass will do her in."

In the parlor, Millie popped up from her spot on the caramel-colored chesterfield sofa and stood beside Holly. "Ignore Jenny, she has a one-year-old at home and doesn't get out much. She likes to let loose when she gets a chance," Millie explained, and Holly nodded. "And you met Vi. She's fantastic. Vi's actually the person who hired me to finish the reno on this house."

"You've done all this?" Holly knew Millie was an interior designer, but she hadn't had a chance to see any of her work in person until now. Standing in a magnificent parlor that featured intricate woodwork and painted mouldings, a modern brass and crystal chandelier hanging from a plaster medallion on the ceiling, and a large stone fireplace, Holly felt like she had been transported to an easier time. A time when wearing frilly dresses and bows in her hair was the norm, and evening drinks with the ladies wasn't a special occasion. "I love it."

Millie giggled. "There are two rooms in this house that I didn't have anything to do with. This is one of them." She bumped Holly who wanted to remove the foot from her mouth. "I'm only teasing you. America and her husband Leo had a great start to the renovation but needed some extra help to get things wrapped up. They are so busy. America is a writer, and they own the Foundry."

"Oh, my goodness." Holly slapped her forehead. "Why didn't I realize that!"

Millie nudged her shoulder. "You're an out-of-towner."

"I live in Elizabethtown, literally a couple miles away from here," Holly said. "And do I need to remind you, you're an out-of-towner too?"

"Maybe I was for a while, but I've been here for months longer than you," Millie said with a smirk that indicated she had won this round. "I know things now."

Vi joined them standing beside the fireplace. "You know what they say about small towns?"

"Where everyone knows everything and everybody?" Holly answered, confident she was correct.

"Small towns are made up of big dreams," Vi said and winked. "I only ever lived in one place, until I came here almost two years ago. I could have never opened a boutique like the one I have now in the city. There are about a thousand shops, all competing for the same customers. Rent is outrageous, for anywhere good anyway, and the chance of succeeding there and keeping one's mental stability intact is low."

"So, the Cove, huh?" Holly asked.

"Tell me why you chose to open your creamery here and not in E-town, or anywhere else for that matter?" Vi asked with genuine curiosity not as someone trying to undermine or manipulate her in some way like Holly might expect her own mother would do.

"Economic growth potential is the reason on the books at the bank," Holly said and looked at her lime green strappy heels hoping to see a different answer there. "And my parents would only back me if I moved closer to home. Is that silly?"

Vi put a hand on Holly's forearm where it was crossed in front of her stomach. "No, dear. It's not silly. It's realistic, and there is not a thing wrong with that."

"She's right," Millie said and handed Holly and Vi glasses of rosé. "You've got to start somewhere. Why not here?"

"Cheers to that!" Holly said. They clinked their glasses and sipped the sparkling pink wine. "Vi, are you going for the grant money?"

"I'm all set, and I'd rather it be awarded to someone who really needs it."

"You're not the secret benefactor, are you?" Millie asked.

Vi choked on her drink a little and smiled. "No. But I know who it is, which is another reason I'm stepping out of the running. What about you?" Vi said as they were joined by Thandie.

Holly nodded. "I could really use it. My parents are tiring of supporting my whims. So, the faster I can be self-supporting, the better for us all. My mother really wants me to go into the business with her, meet a nice man from the country club, and be just like her."

"What's her business?" Vi asked. "I gather from your previous statement that your father is in finance."

"He's a banker. My mother owns H&B Farms. She raises racing horses."

"I know it. Horse and Bridle Farms?" Jenny said, overhearing their conversation from the sofa. "My husband's family owns Townsend's. We have the farm on the far side of the county."

"How have we never met? Surely, we would have run into each other at local events." Holly said.

"I don't like all the pomp, plus my husband's brother raises the horses. We raise the babies," Jenny said.

"Did I hear you say babies, as in plural?" America said as she reentered the parlor.

Jenny shook her head. "I'm not pregnant again. But I won't lie. Cam and I have been talking about trying for another baby soon."

"Like tonight?" America teased. "I mean, look at you. If he doesn't want this, then I don't know if it'll ever happen." Jenny showed off her outfit, a slinky wrap-dress the color of raspberry jam. "I'd have a baby with you looking like that."

"America," Vi scolded.

"What? She's hot." America giggled at herself.

This group of women, all fiercely confident in who they were, fascinated Holly. She hoped to be like them someday instead of pretending and hiding behind the girly persona she had built for herself. The fact was, she had always been a girly-girl, even on the farm, but she had begun to use it as a shield against people who consistently undervalued her. At some point, her frilly dresses and red lipstick had become her whole personality.

While all the women present that night were beautiful, Holly wondered if any of them silently struggled with self-doubt like she did.

A knock rattled the front door and broke Holly's train of thought. America put down her glass and an unopened bottle on the marble coffee table. "Food's here." She stepped out of the room for a moment and returned with an older woman wearing a flowy white eyelet dress, and a giddy Alfonso carrying a three-tiered tray wrapped in yellow cellophane. "You can put it there on the table."

"*Buonasera*," he said and placed the tray where America had indicated. Standing back, he took in the women. "Wow. So much beauty in one place."

"See, he gets it." America joked. "Thank you, Alfonso. Put it on my personal account, okay?"

"I charge free for this view." Alfonso fanned himself and pantomimed fanning the women.

"Oh, stop it. You'll make us all blush and fall in love with you instead of our husbands," Vi said and put her arm around the chef. "What are the guys up to tonight?"

"Alfonso no tell." He zipped his lips shut. "Okay. I tell a little."

"I told you he can't keep anything to himself," Millie whispered to Holly. "I bet they're out plotting against you."

"We paint and build shelves."

"Promise to keep Pa clean. I don't want him tracking in paint all over the floors again," the older woman with silver hair said. "You know I just had them varnished."

"How dirty can he get, Carol?" America said.

Carol laughed. "That man is like a magnet to anything greasy or grimy. If there's a mess, he'll find it."

"You're helping at Teddy's?" Holly blurted out and immediately regretted bringing him up.

"*Si*. And clean windows." Alfonso stared her down and raised one eyebrow practically to his hair line. He knew about what she and Millie had done.

The whole room stilled, and the women looked at each other for answers at the Italian's change in demeanor from jovial to serious. She shrugged as though she was at just as much of a loss as they were.

America finally broke the tension. "I'm sure whatever you boys are doing, will be a good time. Do me a favor and make sure Cam doesn't get too crazy tonight. He has a special job to do at home later."

"America Thorpe! You stop that right now," Vi reprimanded her again.

Alfonso, not understanding, grinned and nodded. "Alfonso go now," he said and removed the cellophane from the snacks before leaving.

"What the heck was that about?" Thandie asked. "I work with him every day, and I've never seen him get so intense so fast."

"It was a misunderstanding," Millie said.

"It wasn't," Holly corrected, ready to finish her story. "Teddy, he's opening the chocolaterie across the street from me." Holly sat on the edge of the marble table and took a tiny triangle cucumber sandwich. "Let's just say, we're taking winning the grant money seriously. I may have painted over his window sign and stolen his workers one day."

"And what has he done to you?" Millie asked, knowing the answer full well.

Holly considered for a moment. "Nothing actually." Guilt began to twist in her gut, but she ignored it. "That's how I know I'll beat him."

"Please tell me you're done tormenting that nice man?" Thandie said.

"Not in the least. He's expecting his shipment of cocoa beans in a couple days, and I plan to put up a roadblock that will have his driver snaking around the entire county," she laughed. Alone. "I'm afraid he won't be getting his beans in time." Holly shoved a whole sandwich quarter in her mouth, wishing the chewing would ease her conscience.

"If I were you, I'd take things down a notch. You don't want to do anything you'll regret," Millie said. "You know I'm your ride or die, but this might be crossing the line."

Holly nodded. Maybe Millie was right—she usually was. She asked herself, if sabotaging her competition was the only way she could win, was it really a win at all? Perhaps she did need to cool it. Teddy had been nothing but kind to her, and she didn't wish to end their flirty and budding relationship over something silly like spray paint.

No matter how much she wanted him, however, she wanted to get out from under her parents' control more. "Let's just talk about something else."

CHAPTER 10

To say that Theodor was a city-kid was the understatement of a lifetime. The truth was never more evident as he pushed through the lower pine branches and undergrowth of what he could only describe as a haunted forest. Haunted, not because of any particular creepy folk-story about the area's history, but from the lingering fog playing tricks in the glow of the fading moonlight. Like a scene from a Robert Frost poem, the sky was dark, but for the waning-moon hanging below the fog and kissing a distant hilltop.

Theodor, having departed his cabin at the Foundry under cover of darkness, hiked to the location of Blake Holly Hollis' latest attempt to thwart him. He'd come prepared wearing his cargo pants that he'd never worn for any outdoor pursuits, and a crisp navy-blue T-shirt. He had his nosy friend, Alfonso, to thank for the advance notice of her subterfuge. When Alfonso had delivered some food to girl's night, he had inadvertently overheard Holly boasting about stopping Theodor's bean delivery. Some detective work by America's husband, Leo, revealed the site. Theodor possessed the other crucial piece: he knew exactly when the truck would be passing this stretch of road.

He could have just called the delivery company and had them go another way from the start, but he needed to catch Holly in the act. He didn't even care how she came to know about his delivery. It didn't matter whether she overheard the information or sought it out. She had decided to use what she knew to hurt him, and he planned to chastise her for being so rotten. The look on her face when he caught her would be the cherry on top.

His plan rested on catching her in the act and stopping her from interfering with traffic, while Alfonso waited to receive the shipment back at his shop. His patience was rubbed thin, but he was looking forward to keeping her occupied and getting to the bottom of why she was acting the way she was.

Stomping over the tender new growth of a leafy bush, he reached the side of the road that bordered the wooded area. Skirting the road on the other side, he could hear the soft rolling water of a stream. Up ahead, an elbow in the path left only one other way for the delivery truck to turn if necessary. This was where she would be. He was certain.

Nearby, an ancient looking stone wall cut a line between the trees and invited him to sit while he awaited Holly's arrival. He brushed some loose material off the stones and plopped down, removing his phone from his pocket. He checked the time and opened his favorite word game app while he waited.

He was only one word into his game when a twig snapped nearby. He froze and strained to hear another sound. Her giggle gave her away. She was close. He could almost smell her vanilla-scented shampoo through the fog but was unable to see her form.

He stood and leaned in the direction where he thought the sound came from, like her infectious laugh called to him. If her crazy wasn't so cute, he might be more cross with her, but he suspected there was more underpinning her actions. Did she crave independence the same way he was screaming inside for his own? Whether she knew it yet or not, they were two of the same kind. He had fallen for the woman she had been on the train, and he held onto the belief that the real Holly would show back up if he kept showing up for her.

He came around a large tree trunk and stepped directly into Holly's path. She became a statue; no fight or flight at seeing him standing there, as though he might not actually see her if she stayed still. There was no mistaking her for any other woman, and he let the ramifications fully sink in for her. He leaned his back against the tree trunk and plucked a strand of long grass that tickled his fingers by his side. Waiting, while she likely decided how she was going to lie her way out of this one, he played with the grass in his hand and glued his eyes to hers.

"Fancy meeting you here," she said with a shrug of her shoulder and tilt of her beautiful long neck. The orange traffic cones in her arms were hardly visible against her equally obnoxious safety vest and white shirt.

"I have to give it to you, you really commit to a bit, don't you? But are we going to act like this is a totally normal thing to happen in the forest before dawn?" he asked.

She stomped and grunted. "How'd you find out I'd be here?"

"I'll never reveal my sources."

"It was Millie, wasn't it?"

He shook his head, and a chuckle filled his throat at knowing she was frustrated. He liked seeing her on her heels. For once, she wasn't in control here. "I can't let you do this."

Holly looked around him and then behind her. "I'm just out for an early morning stroll. What are you doing out here?"

"I'm here for you."

"Creepy, and no thanks," she said, dismissing him, and moved towards the road.

Theodor captured her wrist before she passed by and pulled her towards his body. "Blake Holly Hollis …" He wanted to beg her to stop this game she was playing right now, but he felt the tension crawling like spiders under his skin. "You like this." It wasn't a question. He saw it now in the flicker of light in her eyes, the same flash as he had seen at the dock their first evening together when they nearly kissed.

She released the cones. Heavy plastic crashed against the forest floor as she used both hands to squirm away from him. Her struggle was ineffective, only managing to bring her body closer into his arms as though she hadn't even been trying to get away. If this rendezvous wasn't so damn sexy, he might have thought he was scaring her, but she wasn't scared. She was excited by the tryst. And so was he.

The mouse was chasing the cat, and the cat was purring in his grasp. Tiny little shocks shot around his body, and sparks ignited his fingertips wherever he connected with her skin. Holly leaned into him, completely pliable in his arms. Her wet lips glistened, and he never wanted to taste something more. This wasn't the first time he craved her. No, from the first moment she laughed with him on the train, he'd pictured himself holding her this way, feeling her full, strawberry lips against his, and playfully twisting her blonde ponytail in his hands.

Her questionable actions towards him were the only thing holding him back now. She had to be the one to make the next move, to stop playing him and start being with him. "What do you want, Holly? Because I don't know if I can keep doing this. It's torture."

She closed her eyes and craned up on her toes, bringing her mouth dangerously close. Her breath cooled his skin and gooseflesh pricked up on his neck and arms at their proximity. She had him pinned against the tree with no answer to his query. Flipping the tables, Theodor pulled her lower back in and crushed her against his body. He spun around and pressed her back against the warm trunk, her toes barely reaching to the pine straw ground.

Theodor spoke into the silky skin below her ear. "I won't ask you again." Her breath caught and he knew what effect he was having on her. Her reaction was an answer in itself, almost.

"Teddy," she whispered back. Hearing her sigh his name, the name only she called him, nearly undid him. If he wasn't such a gentleman, he might have taken liberties right there. "I want … I don't know what I want."

Theodor shoved himself back from the tree and removed himself from her intoxicating scent. He ran his fingers through his loose hair, wanting to pull it out, and settled on twisting his locks into a knot at the top of his head. "You can't honestly stand there and tell me that there's nothing between us." He drew air deep into his belly, hoping to cool the irritation in his heart.

"You're right. I can't," she said and stepped towards him.

"What?"

"I can't tell you there's nothing between us." Holly threaded her right fingers through his left and snaked her free arm around his neck, bringing her face to within a hair's breadth of his. "I can't get you out of my mind. I spend more time looking for any glimpse of you standing in your shop than I spend looking around mine. And at night … I just wish this wasn't so hard."

"It doesn't need to be, Holly." Theodor appreciated her brief affair with the truth. "Can we agree to no more games?"

"I can't promise you that," she said and rested her lips on his, though he hesitated to give in.

Backing away, "I can't keep doing this with you, Holly."

"You don't understand—"

"What don't I understand? I understand perfectly that you want nothing more than to win. I understand that you have no self-control or desire to know when you've gone too far, like causing my ingredients to be delivered late, vandalizing my store windows, or stealing my workers—"

"I … I don't want to be that person, but if you only knew—"

"What I know is despite everything you've done, I like you, but I'd rather be nothing than whatever this currently is."

"I like you too," she said so softly that if not for the still forest, he might not have heard her.

He did hear her. "I know," he said back in a hushed tone. "I just needed you to say it." Theodor wrapped his arms around her waist until no space existed between their bodies. "Can we end this whole enemy's thing and skip right to the lovers part?"

"I want to, I really do, but I have to win that money."

Theodor threw his hands in the air. "Even if you beat me, there's a half-dozen other shops that are vying for the same things. But somehow, I am the only person receiving your efforts. Why me?"

"I don't know," she said with a hitch in her voice. "I hadn't really considered them."

"Consider this, I haven't spent a moment since we met thinking of much else than the way you would fit in my arms, like this." He took her by the waist and lifted her to his chest. Her legs wrapped around him and her arms folded together behind his neck. She fit better than he imagined, which must have surprised her too by the way she stilled and held her breath. "Now kiss me like you mean it, and let's be done with this game." Their lips touched like magnets and the whole world illuminated around them.

"Hands up!" a female voice shouted. "Now!"

Theodor released Holly to the ground, and they faced the source of the bright headlights. Two squad cars lit them up from the road and two officers approached. "Everything will be okay," he whispered to her.

"You're under arrest." One of the cops came around him and slapped cuffs on his right wrist. Pulling his arm down, she added the left wrist behind his back and began directing him through the woods. "You have the right to remain silent. You have the right to an attorney—"

"What am I being arrested for? You can't do this!" Holly argued with the other police officer.

Theodor twisted around to see her struggling with the handcuffs. "Just do what they say. I'll get us out of this."

The cop had continued reading him his rights, though it was all a blur while he was focused on Holly. She was placed in the other squad car, and he wondered if she was just as confused and scared as he was. A million past decisions played in his mind during the short trip to the pokey, but he was no closer to figuring out what he had done to deserve to be arrested as he sat squished in the backseat of the vehicle.

CHAPTER 11

WHEN HOLLY HAD PLANNED OUT HER DAY, GOING TO JAIL WAS NOT on the schedule. How could she be so stupid? Not that she did anything wrong, but that she got caught doing the wrong she didn't do. One thing was for certain, if she ever found out that Teddy had anything to do with them getting arrested, she would have his head on a candy skewer.

No, that was too extreme, even for her, but she would definitely do something to make him pay!

She had to admit that neither of them would be there if she hadn't decided to take things too far in the first place. Only two evenings prior, Millie had convinced Holly to cool her hijinks, and Holly had totally intended to at first.

However, yesterday's voicemail from her mother played over and over again in her mind. Her mother's sweet tone was the opposite of the devastating blow her message delivered. "Until your decisions are more in line with the expectations of your family name, you will no longer have access to family funds," Holly said aloud in a voice like her mother's.

The irony wasn't lost on her that the one person whom she wished to confide and find comfort in, was the same person she had just gotten arrested with. Even if she somehow managed to explain her actions, she wasn't delusional. There was little hope that he would forgive her now. Was it she who needed forgiving? If she hadn't been delayed by his sexy plea in the woods, she would have been in and out of there in no time.

Teddy had been booked before her, which was the only time she had seen him since they were dragged out from the woods. She wondered where they had taken him afterwards and imagined him sitting in a cold gray room with one of those fancy two-way mirrors and a stale cup of coffee.

Coffee … She could go for a cup right about now. The morning sun spilled inside the police station windows and indicated the time was likely around eight or nine o'clock. Not that it mattered. No one would even miss her for hours, and she hadn't been given her one phone call yet.

Luckily, the long wait time provided a chance to consider who she would contact. Millie was the obvious choice, except she was out of town for the next couple days sourcing the last furniture and fixtures for America's house renovation. After her parents cut her off yesterday, there was no way she was going to call them for help either. Teddy was a nice guy and would get her out if he could, but she was pretty certain that someone in jail can't bail out someone else in jail. So, that option was out. Holly slumped against the wall. "I guess I'm here forever. Just call me Pen from now on, since that's where you can find me."

She heard Teddy's chuckle before he came into view. *Why is he in such a good mood?* His grin could not have been any wider; a smirk she wanted to wipe off his face at the first opportunity. His sprightly eyes glowed in the sunlight, like he had indeed gotten that coveted cup of coffee. Stale or not, she would take one if offered.

The officer slid open the gate and directed him inside. At the sight of Holly, his smirk soured, causing her to swallow hard. When the gate closed, she instructed Teddy to turn so that his cuffs could be removed. "Get comfy, Saint Theo. They're processing your request now."

Rubbing the reddened depressions around his wrist, Theodor sat on the floor across from Holly.

"Saint?" she asked from a narrow bench built into the concrete wall.

"Apparently, I'm well behaved, they were teasing me about how polite I was," Teddy said and looked at his feet, not at her. "Trespassing, huh?"

"I can't believe we're in here. This is all your fault!"

Her accusation got his attention, and he looked up at her. "Mine?"

"Yes. If you hadn't distracted me with all that ..." she stopped herself from saying anything about the way she had kissed him. "I would have done what I needed to do and been gone before anyone was the wiser." She knew she was partly right and crossed her arms for effect.

"You mean, if I hadn't distracted you from the *other* crime you were attempting to commit," he growled.

"Shush. You want me to get in trouble for that too?"

"Just admit it. You got caught doing something illegal while doing something else illegal." He smirked wryly like he had won this round.

"Wipe that off your face," she said.

"Or what? You'll come over here and do it for me? Be my guest."

She grunted and stomped her foot against the cold floor. "What happened to that whole sexy act in the woods?"

"You think I'm sexy?" he teased sarcastically and crossed his legs out in front of him as though he had no cares in the world, which irritated her more.

"I didn't say that. I said it was an act." Inside she was throwing a fit. She was so confused. One minute he's pinning her against a tree, breathing her in and stirring a desire in her that she had never felt before, and the next, he's indifferent to their plight. "I thought you liked me?"

"That was before you got us arrested." He gave another irritated smirk.

"And why are you so happy?"

"Trust me, honey, it has nothing to do with you." Teddy said with a taunting shake of his head. "This whole day is just one big joke. It has to be, because there's no way this is how this works. I'm a lawyer, remember."

"It's not a joke to me. How do I know this whole thing wasn't one big set up from you?"

"Why would I—"

"To get back at me," she shot back. "To teach me a lesson. I don't know." Voicing her accusation out loud made her paranoid rambling sound ridiculous even to her own ears. There was one way to find out. "Why don't you tell me how you did it, then. How did you get us arrested for trespassing?"

"I don't know what you're talking about. And for that matter, I can't believe you would think I would risk my future to take you down. I'm not like you, Blake Holly Hollis. I would never do the kinds of things that you've been doing to me." He stood and walked to the bars. "I wish we were never told about this grant money, and we could just go back to when you were charming and got me out of my shell."

She recoiled at the realization that she had cut him deep. "I meant to be having fun."

"Fun? That's what you call trying to delay my opening? Believe it or not. I *need* this grant money. I have to succeed at this or… or I'm finished. I'll have nothing to fall back on. You don't even need it. This is just sport for you."

"For your information. I had decided not to reroute your delivery truck until …" she paused and considered whether to tell him about the voicemail she got from her mother yesterday or not.

"Until what? What happened to make you pump the brakes and then why did you go through with it anyway?"

She stood and joined him beside the blue painted metal bars and rested her hands through two slats. "Can I tell you something?" she said, and he shrugged. "Now, you believe it or not. I do like you. I just wish we weren't competing for the same thing. Do you know how hard it is for me to trust you, or anyone, who wants to see me fail?"

He looked at her with glassy eyes. "I don't want to see you fail. I just really need to win. There's a difference. And yes, I thought your antics were innocent enough, like when you distracted my workers with delicious pizza. But then you vandalized my windows, which was borderline for me. Then I found out you were planning to redirect my supplies and possibly ruin my chances of opening my shop in time to even win the money. Until that moment, I believed you were just a girl, having a good time. I even thought you were toying with me as a twisted form of flirtation."

"Teddy, I was, you're right—"

"Stop," he said and put a finger over her lips. His firm flesh warmed her skin, and she found herself without breath. "I'm tired of your games, and you've made it difficult for me to ever trust you again. And as for that grant money, don't even think for a second that you're going to win it after all this."

"But I need it. Teddy, you don't understand. My parents ... they—" She couldn't bring herself to admit that she was on her own, that her mother had pulled one last string with that voicemail to force Holly into a life she didn't want. Everything hinged on the success of her shop now. The last thing Blake Holly Hollis wanted was to appear pathetic to the man standing beside her.

"I have difficult parents too, Holly, but I'm not going to destroy you in order to release my frustrations about them. I told you on the train that I was their greatest disappointment. So yeah, I want to win that money too and prove to them I am so much more than they thought me to be."

"It's no excuse, I suppose."

"You're darn right, it's not," Teddy said and looked away from her down the hallway. "This was the last thing I needed right now."

"You think I want this?" she said and pawed at his shoulder.

"Obviously, or you wouldn't have plotted against me in the first place." Teddy removed her hand from his shoulder. "I'm done."

"But … that kiss," her skin warmed just thinking about it.

"I was trying to distract you from your plan. It worked." Teddy chuckled without humor. "As for that agreement to calm things down? Well, that was before we ended up in jail for trespassing."

Words ricocheted around her mind. All the things she wanted to say to ease her guilt refused to coalesce into sentences, and she gave up. Nothing he said was particularly wrong, and everything he articulated was the truth no matter how much she disliked hearing it. His cold shoulder and tense jaw made it clear that he had slipped away from her. Only now, did she see how much she wanted to have him.

"Saint Theo," a voice rang down the corridor. "Congratulations, you're cleared to leave." The female cop stood in front of the doorway and let him pass. This time, no cuffs were dangled in his face, and no chains rattled. He didn't even look back at her as he made his way down the corridor.

"Wait! Teddy, you can't leave me in here. I haven't had a chance to call anyone. What am I going to do?" She pleaded for him to turn to her. He paused and glared over his shoulder, and she applied a soft smile and sorry eyes to her face. "Teddy?" She shrugged; scared that she was all alone again.

"Actions have consequences, my dear. I hope you learn from yours."

The bars slammed shut against each other and sent vibrations through the floor. She leaped towards him and shoved her arms through the cracks. He was just out of reach and the cop gave a warning with her eyes—the way a mother looks at a toddler and the child knows they're about to be in trouble.

"I'll never forget this, Saint Theo!"

"I bet you won't! I'm pretty unforgettable," he shouted into the air without even turning his head.

"Come on, Teddy! You're really going to leave me here. Seriously?" She put on her saddest sounding pouty voice, the one that always worked to get her way with her father, but this time, she got nothing but shouts from another holding cell telling her to pipe down.

She plopped down onto the bench seat and stared at the place where Teddy had been sitting. Hurt that he had blamed her, when it was both of them trespassing where they shouldn't have been—out there in the woods—his hands on her body, playing in her hair.

"Ugh!" she cried out and stomped around the ten-by-ten space. Every thud of her heel let out a small modicum of frustration. She just wanted to be mad—at Teddy, at her parents, at herself—but all she could do was feel the lingering thrill of the way he had touched her. She was mad that even after their fight, she wanted him more than ever. She needed to get out of there fast.

"Blake Hollis. Phone call," the cop said and not a moment too late as she was about to descend into lunacy.

CHAPTER 12

In addition to Theodor's hungry stomach vibrating with growls in his belly, his phone was buzzing with an angry rhythm too. He took his ringing phone from a generic gray bin where he had placed his personal belongings upon booking. He took a deep breath before answering his dad's call. "Hi, Dad." Theodor didn't get any more words out before the yelling began.

"Do you know what strings I had to pull to get you out of there?"

"Dad, please. It wasn't my fault—"

"Do you know how often I hear that in my courtroom? I may be a good judge of the law, but I have misjudged you for far too long, thinking you would pull yourself together—"

"I am pulling myself together. I'm opening my new shop in a couple of weeks. No thanks to the girl that got me arrested."

"There's a girl? I see. And I've heard everything I need to hear about the situation."

"It's not like that. You're not being evenhanded here," Theodor tried to explain but was cut off again.

"I'm your father. I don't have to be anything. What I am is disappointed, once again. So, you run along and play with your little chocolate bars and don't you dare call me to bail you out again."

"Dad, I was working a deal. You didn't need you to do anything."

The line went dead.

That's when he looked up and saw two cops shaking their heads at him. "Don't you judge me too," he said and placed his wallet and phone in his pants pocket. He retrieved his Peugeot timepiece and slid the gold band over his hand. Last, he replaced his favorite hair elastic—the one he was forced to remove when getting his photo taken—on his wrist.

"You're free to go, Saint Theo," the female officer said, but he knew the drill from attending a criminal law class and waited at the exit door for her to buzz him out to the lobby while wondering how his dad knew about the arrest anyway.

Teddy stopped at a bank of vending machines. He scanned the selection for whatever had the most caffeine and settled on Big Buzz energy drink. *Whatever that is.* He retrieved his credit card from his wallet and shoved it in the slot. He pressed the corresponding button, and nothing happened. "Oh, come on!" The side panel shuddered under the force of his palm, and he bumped the glass with his hip. That's when the scrolling word, *DECLINED*, caught his eye. "You've got to be kidding me." His dad wasn't playing around this time, it seemed.

With no caffeine, no money, and no way to get home, he passed through the outside doors and cringed at the bright, mid-morning sun. Taking a deep breath of clean air, cooler and more pleasant than the atmosphere had been inside the jail, he filled his lungs with the essence of freedom.

No amount of relief at being out could squash the anger that was strangling his heart. He hated his father for cutting him off, and he hated Holly for causing him to feel so mad and disappointed.

The full breath allowed him a moment to scan his

surroundings. That's when he spotted Alfonso sitting on the hood of the red truck. Theodor walked with purpose and pointed his finger at Alfonso. "You called my dad? I was taking care of it. I even had a deal worked out to get us both out for free."

Alfonso put his hands up in surrender. "Alfonso not know this and call mamma."

"That's even worse," Theodor said and stopped in his tracks. "She's the last person that actually likes me."

"Alfonso like." He held a hand over his heart and then pointed it to Theodor. "Alfonso. Theodor. Bros, no?"

"Yes, Alfonso, we're friends. And thank you for getting me out, however you went about it. I'm grateful to not be stuck in there with her for one more minute."

"Holly?"

"Who else?" Theodor looked back at the building's side door where he'd exited. "I left her in there. I tried to cut a deal and talk my way out of it, but there was nothing else I could do but wait for the judge to decide." He opened the passenger side door. "Plus, she deserves to stay in there a little longer for what she was going to do. Speaking of that, did you get the delivery?"

"*Si*," Alfonso climbed in the front seat and slammed the door. "What now?"

"Drive. I need to get to the shop. I have more work to do than ever. My father turned off the money spigot and now I have to win that grant money to keep my shop going. I can't afford anything else going wrong."

Alfonso put the truck into reverse but was halted by a passing car honking a horn behind him. He wasted no time throwing the truck into park and diving out the door, shouting something in Italian and flailing his arms and hands in the air. Theodor rolled down the window and pulled his upper half through the opening, sitting on the narrow ledge. A woman got out of the car, the wind blew her dark hair in front of her face and shrouded her features, but she shouted right back at Alfonso.

The high-pitched voice was unmistakable. "Hey, Millie. Here for a conjugal?" Theodor teased once he knew for sure who the woman was.

"Very funny." She rolled her eyes and approached him. "You know I told her to back off of all this, and I thought she listened to me for once. I can't believe she went ahead with her harebrained idea."

"You've got to be kidding me. You knew what she was planning and didn't stop her?"

"You act like I'm in charge of her. Holly has always had a mind of her own, just ask her parents who cut her off yesterday." Millie slapped herself in the forehead. "That's why she did it. Now, her creamery is her last shot to make it on her own."

"I don't care if she was told to do it at gun point, she went too far. And what makes her reason so special? This business is my only chance too, but you don't see me sabotaging her at every corner just to win a few bucks."

Alfonso came around and whispered into Millie's ear causing her to look at him with sad eyes. "You've been cut off too? That's not great, but now you'll have to suck it up like the rest of us and work for a living instead of relying on daddy."

"That's amusing coming from someone defending a rich girl for the same reason."

Alfonso put his body between Theodor and Millie but faced Millie. "No fight like racoons. Get Holly. Alfonso got bro." He nodded with his head towards Theodor as though Millie wouldn't know who he was referring to.

She put her hands up and walked back to her sedan. "Keep him away from me and keep him away from my best friend, will you?"

The two guys stood by and watched as she pulled her car forward and parked in a vacant visitor spot before they got back into the red truck. Theodor's emotions floated over the abyss of his reality. Nothing she said about him needing to work for his own living was wrong. But it's one thing to strike out on your own and another to know you're still in spring training. Until fifteen minutes ago, he was biding time, now he was thrown into the big game of life.

"Alfonso, I think spring training is over. No more Saint Theo. I'm winning the grant money no matter what. Now let's get out of here."

CHAPTER 13

IT WAS STRANGE ENOUGH THAT INSTEAD OF GETTING TO MAKE HER phone call, Holly had been released shortly after Teddy and with no formal charges being filed. The entirety of the event had ended like it had begun; out of nowhere. Stranger still was the sight of her best friend sitting on the hood of her car outside the police station doors. On any other day, Holly knew Millie would come through and bail her out, but she was not expecting her today because Millie was supposed to have been out of town.

"You're a mess," Millie said as she wrapped her arms around Holly. "And you smell like woods and fart."

"My next best-selling flavor." Holly pantomimed a banner in the air above their heads. "How'd you know I was here?"

"I just knew you were going to do something stupid," Millie said as they got into her sedan. "I have a friend in the force who called me. I just don't know why you got yourself in this situation."

"I appreciate you coming. I just wish Teddy had stayed out of it."

"Do you think you would have let someone do what you were about to do to his supplies?" Millie said and cranked the car.

"I suppose not. He's going to hate me forever." Holly buckled her seatbelt, not wanting another mark on her record anytime soon.

"I ran into Teddy and Alfonso a few minutes ago. He didn't seem too pleased with you."

"Like you said, he has every right to be. I was about to do something truly awful had he not stopped me first. We were alone, in the forest, and he asked me to stop playing him. I actually agreed. Not that it mattered since we got arrested anyway." Holly buckled her seatbelt and collapsed it the grey fabric bucket seat. "I still don't know how the trespassing charges got dropped."

Millie shrugged and put the car into drive. "Where to?"

"The creamery."

They headed straight to the shop and got to work, since she was now a day behind her plans. Inside, Holly took hold of a box of merchandise that had been delivered during her time in lock-up and dropped it in the storage room at the back of her shop. Millie picked up another and followed behind Holly.

"I was so shocked to see you today. You were supposed to be in the city with America, picking out furniture." Holly took the box from Millie and stacked the item on top of the first one.

"She got called into work on an assignment, and we rescheduled our shopping trip for later this week."

"Does this mean you're mine for the day? Or what's left of it," Holly said with the sun casting Main Street in bronze hues. "Right now, I can use all the help I can get."

"How long until you open?" Millie said and brought another box to the storage room.

"I'm hoping I can open for the Fourth of July weekend, but that will depend on getting the health inspector out here in time. It seems like a long time, but my to-do list only keeps growing. No matter how many things I cross off, there's more to do the next day. Take all of this merch for instance, I have nowhere to display any of it yet, but I have to store it somewhere for the time being."

Holly placed the last box inside the storage area next to her office and walked back out into her half-done space. The dark green walls and exquisite gilded mouldings looked perfect and were the only thing in the shop that was finished. Her mural was nearly complete, but for the detail work that she hadn't had time to attack yet. In one corner near the front window, she had piled shopping bags full of faux peonies and ivy vines that she planned to hang on the rear wall as a selfie spot. Light fixtures were waiting to be hung, and the floor tile still hadn't been installed. Truth be told, progress had been slow going since she changed her focus from working to winning. She was just glad she had done that bulk of her purchases before her mother cut her off.

With her hands on her hips, Holly took a deep breath and raspberried her lips as she blew the air from her lungs. "Hey, Millie," she sang her friend's name. "What do you know about laying tile?"

Millie's face lit up and her cheeks filled with joy causing Holly to be hopeful that Millie knew a great deal about flooring installation. "I thought you'd never ask."

Holly clapped her hands together. "Do you think we can finish this project tonight? That way I can start moving the tables and décor in here."

"We won't know until we try."

"I appreciate the enthusiasm, Millie."

The girls wasted no time gathering loose items and taking them all to the storage room. Holly filled the office and storage closet to the brim. The larger items, like display cases and bistro sets, would fit nowhere inside, but the sidewalk out front was clean and vacant. She only hoped no one would mind having to walk around her stuff for a few hours.

They moved the smaller pieces of furniture with no issue, until they got to the beast of a display case. "I can't lift this,"

Millie said while straining to move the glass and stone counter. "We're not ever going to get to laying the floor if we don't get this thing out of here."

"Know anyone who could help?" Holly asked and scanned the sidewalk outside for anyone that looked strong enough to assist them. Carol, the older woman she met during girls' night at America's was making her way across the cobblestone road, and a small lady, pushing a baby stroller, came down the other direction.

"Hey, Carol!" Holly flagged her over. "You know anyone who can help us move some of this big stuff?"

Carol looked inside the doors and shook her head like she was thinking. "I could see if Pa and some guys from the Foundry could come help, though it'll probably be a few hours before they can sneak away."

A few hours? Holly was uninterested in waiting that long. She looked at Millie over her shoulder. "Maybe we can slide it with something."

"Thanks anyway, Carol. I think we'll try something else," Millie said. "We're on a mission to get these floors done."

"Alfonso help," a voice said from behind Carol in the doorway. He stood in the double wide space with his arms extending outward to each jamb.

"Looks like you're covered," Carol said. "Best of luck, girls." She patted Alfonso on the shoulder before turning to leave. With a basket of baked-goods hanging on her arm, Carol continued on her way.

A smirk as wide as Alfonso's stance was the siren call to Millie's eyes. "How did you know we need help?" Millie said and, standing on her tiptoes, kissed Alfonso's cheek. "I'm sorry for how I acted at the station earlier. I was just irritated at this one." She pointed at Holly who put her hands up in surrender. Holly knew there was no point in arguing with Millie anymore. "Aren't you supposed to be cooking dinner at the Foundry or helping Teddy?"

"The guests requested cold dinner. All food prepared. Theodor needed bro-power."

Holly joined the pair by the front door. "If you're helping Teddy, then why are you over here and not with your bro over there?"

As he stumbled through an explanation spoken in half Italian and English, and maybe some French thrown in too, he dug into his pants pockets. *"Un momento."* He patted his torso and landed on his chest pocket. "Ah. Note for Holly."

Holly took the scrap of folded brown paper. The outward facing fold was addressed to *BHH* from *Saint*. "It's from Teddy. I'm not reading it." She shoved it back at Alfonso, who stepped away like she was holding the plague in her fingertips. "Fine." She unfolded the paper and scanned the beautiful cursive script. *Now, you're just showing off,* she thought.

"What's it say?" Millie asked and pumped her brows.

"Hey, jailbird. Nice to see you out of the slammer." Holly crumpled the paper and tossed it in the corner. "I mean … what a rotten human being he is."

"Is that fair?" Millie said. "You've been no angel."

Holly huffed. "He's just antagonizing me. What kind of gentleman treats a lady in such a way."

"And what kind of lady steals someone else's workers, vandalizes a storefront, and whatever you call the stunt with the delivery truck? If he's trying to get under your skin, can you really blame him?"

Holly knew her friend was right, but she wouldn't dare say it. Nor would she admit the she had accused him of getting them both arrested just to hurt her. "Get me a piece of paper." She had a note to send of her own.

Millie returned from the office with a stack of pink sticky notes and handed them over. "What are you gonna say?"

With the pen in her hand, she said and wrote the words simultaneously. "You're no saint, Teddy Black. The charges against me were dropped, no thanks to you. I hope your shop burns down when you roast your beans. See you never, loser."

Millie's hand fell on the back of Holly's shoulders. "Are you sure you want to give that to him? He's being cheeky, and that seems mean."

Of course she wanted to say it. Holly folded her square into a triangle, again and again, until it was a tiny, fingernail-sized note. She handed it back to Alfonso. "Can you please give this to your bro? After you help us move this big piece of furniture?"

Alfonso stashed the note in his shirt pocket while shaking his disappointed head back and forth. The slower his head rotated, the more decay she felt inside. Straightening her spine, Holly decided she had no time to feel anything for Teddy Black. She had a list of a thousand things to accomplish before she could let her heart dictate a course to her. "Oh, stop judging me with those smoky, beautiful Italian eyes of yours, and help us get this thing outside."

Alfonso made the task look easy as the three of them worked together to maneuver the large counter out to the sidewalk. They placed it alongside the front windows and out of the way of any pedestrians. "Thank you, Alfonso. And don't forget to give the note to Teddy."

"Are you sure?" Millie said and shook her head at Alfonso. "I wouldn't. Why don't you write something else. Maybe an apology?"

"No." A rift was opening in Holly's heart and distracting her from her goals. She was attracted to Teddy, like a comet hurling towards the sun. His bright light served as a spotlight on all of her insecurities and traumas. The only way to nip this in the bud was to let it go. "Make sure he gets that, Alfonso."

They watched Alfonso walk across the street and Millie put her arm around Holly's waist. "For the record, I think you're making another huge mistake. You shoot from the hip, which normally does you good, but I think you're having a hard time squaring what you want for your future with what's right in front of you."

"What I want is to lay the flooring." Holly chose to ignore Millie rather than internalize any of her words and risk the discomfort that might come from admitting the truth to herself.

Inside, Millie gathered the supplies to lay the floor tiles. "This choice of materials, however, is one of your better decisions, Holly."

Holly had selected the luxury vinyl tiles because they looked like expensive stone and would be the most durable and easy to install option. "Just because I was spending someone else's money doesn't mean I wasn't conscious about the budget."

"It's a smart purchase, if we don't screw up the install," Millie added. "First, we need to unpack the boxes and mix the tiles up, that way if there's any variance in dye-lot, you won't have a patch that looks totally different."

"How do you know all this?" Holly asked as she began to unbox the dark gray and white marbled squares. "Design school?"

"Heck no. HGTV," Millie said and giggled. "I've always wanted to try and do this."

"Amelia Anne! Are you telling me you've never laid tile before?"

"How hard can it be?" She pulled a sheet of paper from one of the boxes and presented it to Holly. "We just have to follow the instructions. Look, these snap together. So long as the first line is straight, it should go together like bam, bam, bam. Instant floor."

Holly seriously doubted it would be an instant floor but decided to go along with her fearless DIY leader. At this point in her day, she had been up for more hours than she thought was natural, been arrested, felt all the emotions one could feel towards a person, and now, she was in crunch time to get the floors done.

Together, the women snapped a chalk line along the front of the shop and another up the center length of the room all the way to the rear. Holly wanted the tiles placed like a checkerboard and on a diagonal to make the room appear larger and more whimsical. Luckily, her plan wasn't thwarted by her ambition and once the first line of tiles was laid, the rest snapped into place with ease.

"Knocky-knock," Alfonso poked his head in the front door with the streetlamp casting a long, chef-shaped shadow across the newly installed flooring. "Note delivery." He tossed a balled-up piece of paper across the room towards Holly where she was crouched down on her knees. The paper bounced like a skipping rock on the lake and rolled to a stop an arm's reach away to her left. "*Buona notte, Signorine*. Alfonso go now."

Millie popped to her feet and ran to the doorway where Alfonso stood. "Are we okay?" She kissed his cheek like she had done earlier and gave a brief hug. Alfonso nodded and returned a kiss on her cheek.

From where Holly was scrambling to reach the note, laid out on her belly, she was unable to hear what else Millie and Alfonso were saying with words, but no words were necessary to see that there was something more romantic happening between them.

Millie giggled and Alfonso's chuckle filled the room. She stood perched like a flamingo with one leg bent and resting against her inner thigh of the other leg. There were more hand gestures than Holly knew what to make of, but she was certain the two were up to something. When he departed, Millie's crimson cheeks gave her feelings away.

"Oh my gosh. You like really like him," Holly teased and sat crisscross. Millie joined her on the floor as she tossed and caught the little paper ball in her palm. "I don't want to read it."

"First, of course I like him …" Millie paused and shook her head. "But we're just friends. I've gotten to see him a lot since working on America and Leo's house reno, that's all."

"Could have fooled me," Holly said and rolled the balled-up note between her fingers. "And the second thing?"

"You *do* want to know what that note says. You're not the only person who can read the room. Do you want me to look first?" Millie presented an open palm and pumped her fingers open and closed. "We don't have all night for you to decide. Give it."

A dozen possible responses ran through her mind. She might have blamed him for being rotten, but she knew she had crossed a line that morning. Even though getting arrested was a wake-up call, she still needed to win the money. She could play nice and not work against him anymore, but she didn't know how her previous actions would impact what was left of their relationship. She tossed the paper to Millie who caught it and wasted no time in unfurling it.

"I shouldn't have written that last note." Holly hung her head in her hands.

"Probably not. That's always been your biggest problem. You act or speak before you really think things over." Millie bit her lips between her teeth and her brows pinched together in the middle.

"What? Millie, what does it say?"

Millie turned the paper around already giggling in her throat.

"'Made you look!' That's all it says." Confusion warped her own face. "What does that mean?"

The answer was standing in the glow of the twinkle-lights strung across the road outside, tapping on the windows. "Made you look!" Teddy yelled through the glass and waved.

By the time she shot to her feet and ran to the door, he turned tail and ran down the street with his little sidekick, Alfonso, trailing behind. She let out a grunt and stomped her feet. "That man drives me crazy. Why do you think he's still teasing me, after everything?"

"Perhaps he's not done with you despite your best efforts."

Holly shrugged and flopped against the floor, harder than she had wanted to, and let out an exasperated sigh.

"That man is your soulmate, you know that right?" Millie tossed the paper back to Holly. "You'll see it eventually, if you don't ruin it first."

"You're one to talk, *signorina*," Holly said in her best Italian accent and threw the paper back.

"Let's just get this done, and you can go back to plotting against that sexy man later."

"Maybe my plotting days are over," Holly said as she considered if she had already dashed any chance of a relationship with Teddy. The way he had pressed her back against the tree and breathed her in, his hands holding her firmly, and his lips ... "I don't know what to do."

"Yes, you do."

Could Holly truly have been wrong about everything? She considered Millie's words, despite her best efforts to ignore them. Holly was the one causing all the problems. Millie was only trying to save her from herself the way a best friend does. "I think I should just focus on making the creamery the best establishment in town, and I'll win the money fair and square."

CHAPTER 14

THEODOR WAS ON A MISSION TO WIN. HE COULDN'T AFFORD TO not be a success at this point. After being arrested, even though it was totally not his fault, his father had cut him off, and he knew his mother would go along with whatever his father dictated.

There was little else his mother cared about than keeping her busy charity gala schedule going. If she spent a fraction of the time that she gave to needy libraries, art exhibits, and political candidates on him instead, Theodor was convinced he would be a more well-adjusted adult than he felt. She was a good mom in the sense that she loved him and provided for all of his physical needs. He had never gone without the best clothing, and their home was a magnificent apartment that overlooked Central Park with a floor to ceiling view from north to south. He was grateful for having a privileged upbringing, but one thing people don't understand about growing up as a rich kid is how life can feel so empty. No number of friends and acquaintances could satisfy the space in his heart reserved for his parents' approval.

Now that it was clear he would never get anything more from his father, he had no choice but to fill that vacuum with his own contentment. His new road was one he would walk confidently and unapologetically, and if that meant the first step was to start by plastering the street with advertisements for his shop, then he would take all night if he needed.

He had used a photo of his storefront windows and made a few changes using photoshop. His shop's sign in the photo now read 'Up State Chocolaterie, for Whenever Your Sweet Tooth Strikes.' He would play fair with Holly, and the other shop owners vying for the money, and get the last laugh when his shop was overflowing with customers.

He slapped one of his flyers beside one Holly had put up a few days earlier on a light pole. His was far more eye-catching with the gold foiled lettering catching the late afternoon sun.

"Take that, Blake Holly Hollis!"

As the words left his mouth, a blonde-ponytailed, pink-ribboned, frilly-dressed woman stepped out of the boutique to his right. He turned and stood behind the post. As narrow as it was, it was nowhere near wide enough to cover more than a sliver of his body. "Shoot," he scolded himself. There was no way she didn't see him hiding there. He had two choices, face her, or skedaddle.

Theodor knew that no matter how much he wanted to get back at Holly, he wasn't cut out to be a vindictive son of a you know what. He hoped his light-hearted teasing would be an olive branch to her. He didn't like what she had done to him, but he did understand her desire to win, especially after learning that her family had cut her off. He was just glad she had tamped down her antics for now.

"Saint Teddy, is that you?" Holly said, and he could hear the tapping of her heels against the pavement as she approached.

Run, he told himself, but he was glued in place. She was on him in the span of three deep breaths and drummed her fingers on his shoulder. Theodor twisted his head and looked at an empty street. Turning his head the other way, Holly's proximity caused him to jump back like she was a rattlesnake. In reality, she was a little scarier than a slithering reptile, though far prettier.

"Made you look," she said in a teasing tone and waved her little fingers. She ripped a flyer from his grasp and read the words. "A chocolate tasting this weekend. Good idea."

"That's it? No sneaky scheme or flirting to try and get under my skin?" he said and snatched his flyer from her fingers more dramatically than he intended. During the motion, he touched the back of her hand for a split second. His fingers tingled. The sensation was enough to send heat around his body and up his neck. If he could just tell his body that she was his nemesis, then perhaps he could cease burning for her. Not seeing her every single day would make it considerably easier to get her off his mind, but the nearness of their shops would make that desire unattainable.

Holly placed a soft hand on his forearm. "Listen, Teddy, I know I went too far with the last stunt, and I promise my troublemaking days are behind me. You just keep planning your chocolate tasting." Holly patted the stack of flyers in his arm.

She was being suspiciously nice. He sighed, desperate for the feeling of freefalling to end. Since the moment he met her, his life had been floating on the breeze and had been picking up speed each day. "I can't read you, and I really don't want to fight with you, Holly." His moment of honesty was met with a side eye and shoulder shrug. "I don't know why, but I can't escape your gravity."

This shut her up. She swallowed and blinked in rapid succession like she was grasping for words; some snide remark that would only serve to disguise her feelings, whatever they were. One thing he was sure about was that he was not the source of her pain. If she allowed him in, he would fight for her, not against her.

"Holly, I meant what I said in the woods the other day."

She shook her head. "I don't recall you saying much." Her

cheek pulled up and scrunched the skin under her eye. It was subtle but he knew she was thinking about that kiss.

"Truce?" he said and wet his lips.

Holly leaned in and placed her mouth near his ear. Her breath cooled his heated skin, and his heart thudded against his ribs while he held a shallow breath. "Would you like that?" her whispered words vibrated through his veins. She kissed his earlobe, letting her soft lips press into his flesh. She backed off and looked at him up and down.

"That's not an answer."

Holly turned and her bag caught the corner of his flyers, pulling the stack out of his hands. Papers scattered all over the sidewalk. "I'm so sorry." She bent down and began gathering loose papers.

Theodor chased a few caught in a gust and met her back at the light pole. "That wasn't on purpose, was it?" He let his hand rest atop hers as she handed the flyers back to him.

"No, but I probably deserved that," she said. "Good luck with your event. I mean it." She turned and walked away, leaving him to wonder whether the nice-girl act was real or not.

CHAPTER 15

HOLLY WOULD NEVER ADMIT IT TO HER MOTHER, BUT SHE WAS made for moments like the one she was about to step into. All her years of media training, etiquette lessons, and countless experiences attending high-profile events aided in boosting her confidence. Her heels scraped the white concrete sidewalk as she stopped in front of the pink Victorian house at the far end of Main Street. Standing beyond the white picket-fence gate, she took in the moment before going in.

Every window glowed with soft yellow light and dozens of guests moved through the expertly designed spaces. She had seen glimpses of America and Leo's home during girl's night, but she had yet to see it completely outfitted. Knowing Millie's taste and attention to details, Holly was sure the home would look spectacular.

Millie waved at Holly through the front bay window and sprinted out the front door towards her. "Boy, am I glad you're here. I can only do small-talk for so long before I want to rip my ears off."

"It's going that well, huh?"

With arms threaded together, the two women strolled the

short distance through the front garden. Holly's heels tapped with each footfall along the brick path and low, boxwood hedges tickled the sides of her exposed calf. An older couple, wearing business suits, walked out of the house. Holly and Millie shuffled to one side of the path and let the guests pass by. The woman smiled and nodded to Millie as she departed.

Millie leaned into Holly. "I just feel so out of my league with these people, like I'm a poser or something."

"I think everyone feels that way when starting something new. But look at all these people who are going to know your name and your business after tonight."

"I have gotten a lot of interest in my design services, which is good," Millie said and smiled.

"This open-house was a brilliant idea, then," Holly said and scanned the guests faces to see if she knew anyone. Luckily, she didn't, but being so close to home meant that there was always a chance to run into an old flame, or grade-school teacher somewhere. She just wasn't prepared to have to explain the whole situation.

"Looking for someone?" Millie asked as they approached the front steps. "A certain chocolatier maybe?"

"What?" Holly said. "I was not actually, but now that you mention him ... no."

"If you say so." Millie laughed. "And this event wasn't my doing. America thought it would be a nice way to thank the community for everything they've done. I'm just mooching off the opportunity."

"Millie, it's not like you're taking credit for something you didn't do. I know you came in halfway through the project, but look at what you've accomplished—"

"You want to see the scrapbook?" Millie said and yanked Holly through the foyer and up the stairs.

Last time she was there, Holly kept to the kitchen and parlor and hadn't ventured anywhere else. At the top of the wooden staircase, a veranda wrapped around the two-story entryway with rooms lining the other side. Millie led her around the walkway where a soft scent of warm vanilla called them to a room at the front end of the house.

"Is this Cinderella's library?" Holly asked and went straight to the shelves filled with books. At the center of the longest wall, candles flickered in the old fireplace box. An oversized gilded mirror hung above the white painted mantel and reflected the position of a small desk on the opposite side of the room.

"I suppose you could say that. It's America's office," Millie said and sat at the desk positioned under the window. "And before you ask, I had nothing to do with this space, it was all America. Well … I rearranged the books and added some new throw pillows to the egg chair."

"It's such a pretty space," Holly said and joined Millie at the desk. "Let's see that scrapbook."

Millie opened the white leather-bound folio and slid it along the desk to where Holly stood. "America was able to get these old photos from the town's archives and make copies. These old black and white ones of this house were taken in 1901."

They flipped through page after page of history. Every iteration of the home had been documented, from original Victorian style to the art deco lead windows in the twenties, and an attempt to change the roofline to a flattop in the sixties. It was repainted in the nineties in a similar pink as it had now, though the fresh color scheme gave the home a whimsical feel.

"It kinda matches my shop, don't you think?" Holly said as they got to the page that showed the most recent renovations. "I can't believe it looked this rough only a couple months ago."

"When Vi hired me, it was right after America and Leo got married and were on their honeymoon. Since all the permits had already been approved, I was able to get to work right away. Honestly, I got pretty lucky with this project since America had done most of the planning. She really just needed me to come in and manage the work."

"I think you do far more than just manage. You have that special thing where you see beauty and know how to make others see it too," Holly said and meant it. "I've always admired you for that."

"Thank you for saying that. And I've always admired you for being able to talk to anyone about anything. I hate events like this."

It was unfortunate that Holly's first reaction to a compliment was to recoil and wonder what the person's motives were, but she knew Millie to be one of the few true souls in her life. She had never lied to Holly as far as she knew and had no reason to suspect she would start now. "Thank you for saying that. And thank you for sticking by my side. I know I'm not the easiest person to get."

"I think it helps that I've known you since you were still picking your boogers. But you're welcome."

Holly threw her arms around Millie's shoulders and embraced her friend, glad to have her back in town to cause trouble with. "Now, show me the rest of the place?"

"And try all the snacks," Millie said and rubbed her tummy.

"Tour first, then food."

They walked around the rest of the upstairs, three bedrooms and two spacious bathrooms. The primary bedroom had vaulted ceilings and exposed beams with a four-poster bed positioned against one wall. Soft white drapes hung at all the windows and a bench seat overflowed with lush cushions. The room was clean, simple, and romantic.

Downstairs, the final space she had yet to see was a masculine study featuring dark wood wainscoting and a clay treatment on the upper third of the walls. Holly ran her fingers across the textured surface. The roman clay was so fine, it felt like silk.

"This is Leo's office, and my favorite part of the house. When

I got here this whole room was stripped down to the studs. I researched similar homes and found that most houses of this size would have had a smoking room. So, I used that as inspiration for Leo's office, and he loves it."

"Who says I do?" A man with blond hair entered behind them through the glass French doors. He put his hand out to greet Holly.

She met his hand. "You must be America's other half."

"Leo. Nice to meet you."

"I'm Holly. Millie's friend. I feel like we've just been missing each other since I got to town a couple weeks ago. I was at the Foundry for the chocolate festival, and I was here about a week ago for girls' night."

"You're opening the creamery down the way?"

"That's right," Holly said with pride dripping off her happy tone.

"And it's going to be sooo good." Millie added, causing Holly to bump shoulders with her.

Leo snapped his fingers. "You know the guy who's opening a chocolate shop across the street from you? I bet you two have a lot in common. I mean you both like sugar."

Holly smiled and prepared a congenial answer. "Mister Black, I believe."

"I can introduce you if you like," Leo said.

"Perhaps, sometime. I'm really quite busy building my business. I appreciate the offer—"

"No need to thank me. Let me get you both something to drink. It's a party after all." Leo exited the office with a bounce in his step.

"He's fun," Holly chuckled and moved towards the window that looked out to a side garden.

"Don't let him fool you, he knows that you and Teddy are well acquainted," Millie said. "He's up to something."

While Holly gazed out, there was a subtle reflection of people coming into the office and greeting Millie. Their conversation faded into the background of her mind as the scene outside pulled her focus. Though night had fallen, the sun gave light to the horizon in shades of bronze and purple and allowed Holly to make out the garden's features. A tall fence of hedges stood in a tight, manicured row while fluffy hydrangeas drooped over a short stone wall abutting a stone path. The path called to her, and she desired to discover what secrets could be hidden at the end.

"You did this, didn't you?" Holly asked Millie with no reply. "Millie?"

In the reflection of the window, she could make out the forms of people moving about. As one came closer, she knew it wasn't Millie.

"Beautiful view," Teddy said from behind her and caused her to spin around. Her defenses engaged at the sound of his voice. He handed her a champagne flute. "Leo asked me to give this to the pretty woman in the office. I suppose he was directing me to you."

She sipped the fizzy Prosecco to buy herself some time while she decided how to react to him. She grinned behind her glass and wondered if Millie's earlier warning to her was too late. There was a chance she had already ruined whatever relationship she could have had with Teddy. She wished she could dislike him, but she didn't. Her brain wanted to focus on the business, but her heart wanted to be wrapped in his arms.

He tilted his head. "You look really pretty tonight," Teddy said and took a drink.

They were far beyond small talk at this point in their relationship which made this interaction feel like sandpaper in her mind. "Thank you. You clean up nicely too." He wore a light blue suit with a white button-down underneath. The top three buttons were left undone, and she spied a hint of chest hair peeking out. Like the garden pathway outside, it beckoned her to explore deeper. The shadow created by his open shirt captivated her imagination.

"What are you looking at?" he said and stole her attention back to his face.

She was looking at how gorgeous he was, but she couldn't say that. He wore his hair loose and smooth making the length appear longer than it had the prior time he had it down at the police station. His dark locks begged to be touched, not just admired. "I—I was just thinking about how much I like the garden outside." She sipped her drink.

Teddy pushed her drink down from her mouth. "Why do you do that?"

"What?" she said and knitted her brows like she was confused when in reality, she didn't want to admit to something unnecessarily.

"Deflect from anything real. You were lost in thought imagining what I look like without my shirt on. Admit it."

She shoved the glass into his chest forcing him to take possession of it. "I was not." He captured her hand along with the glass against his body. His dark pools took her captive. She was helpless to look anywhere else and heat climbed her neck. "Teddy," she whispered and swallowed hard.

"I like how you say my name," he said and kissed her cheek. "And despite how vexing you are, I can't shake this feeling."

Her eyes shut and she breathed him in. Cocoa and cedar filled her head and was more intoxicating than the Prosecco could ever be.

"I see you found her." Leo came in and saved her from the embarrassment of letting her defenses down any more than she already had.

Teddy's body blocked her from Leo, and he stepped back a few inches, waiting for her to reset her posture and facial expression. Wanton desire gave way to rehearsed manners.

Teddy turned to face Leo, standing in the doorway. A few seconds was all it took for them both to go back to pretending.

"She's as beautiful as you alleged," Teddy said.

Leo ran his hands through his blond waves. "I told ya' you'd like each other."

"Actually, Leo ..." Holly stood aside creating a sort of conversation triangle. "I'm sorry for misleading you slightly, but Teddy and I already know each other. I didn't mean to misrepresent anything to you. I was just keeping things professional."

"I understand. Everyone knows everyone in a small town. I should have assumed you two would know each other too. Here I was thinking I finally got the chance to introduce some new folks."

"Is that so," Holly said. "Millie said you know very well about Teddy and me."

Leo bit his lips inside and nodded slowly like a kid caught with his hand in the proverbial cookie jar. "Guilty." He chuckled in his throat.

"In any case, if you're looking to introduce me to someone new, I'm sure there's folks I don't know yet."

"Have you met Pa, Carol's husband?" Leo asked. "He's the man in town that gets stuff done. If you ever need anything, he's the guy to call on."

"Not yet, but he sounds like someone I should get to know." *Now that I don't have my parents to fall back on*, she thought.

"He's great," Teddy said.

"Well, I look forward to the introduction," Holly said.

"I'll leave you to it." Leo smiled and left, greeting another guest entering the foyer behind him.

Once alone again, their soft laughter livened the space. "Wouldn't things be so much easier if we were on the same team?" Teddy said and handed a nearly emptied glass back to her. "Don't deflect."

She was beginning to like the way he called her out on her bull and was tempted to drop her glass and jump into his arms. He made her feel more seen than anyone she had ever met, which is probably why she was so uncomfortable with the idea. However, the question lingered; would he feel the same once he saw the real her, the whole her; the version of herself that hid behind lipstick and ruffles. The risk was too great while she had a to-do list a mile long and ambitions to achieve. She downed the last of her drink and placed the glass on the acrylic desktop. "I can't let you in right now. No matter how charming you are."

His smirk softened into an emotionless expression as though he deflated.

"I'm sorry, Teddy—"

"Don't." He stepped around her and walked out without so much as a secondary glance.

Was she blowing something that could be magical, good even? "Wait, what are you doing here anyway?" She chased after him.

"I catered the desserts." Teddy walked towards the kitchen, his shoulders slumped forward a little and his steps lazy.

Holly halted her pursuit and reminded herself to stop going places with Millie. Somehow, Teddy was everywhere Millie was, and if Holly continued on her path to the kitchen, she suspected she would find a certain Italian chef lingering around too. "Everyone knows everyone." With no one to confide in at present, Holly slipped out the front door and made for her shop. There was no point in heading back to Millie's to crash, there was too much to get done.

CHAPTER 16

THEODOR WOKE UP, SLUMPED OVER THE COLD METAL TABLE IN HIS shop's kitchen. Since the open house, he hadn't left his store but to take a shower and change his clothing. He had roasted a small batch of cocoa beans earlier in the week, as a test, but he was in crunch time to get his inventory ready for opening day. A week to go until the Chamber would do their walkthrough meant he had no time to waste.

With the storefront approaching the finishing phase of construction, he placed his focus on the part of the process he loved best: chocolate. There was something so relaxing about working the cocoa with his hands, nurturing the rich liquid and creating something beautiful and delicious. The method he employed was half science, half art, and both aspects challenged him in ways that excited him. Practicing law could never provide the same feeling.

His enthusiasm couldn't be explained in mere words, he had to show it, which was one obstacle in the way of winning his parents' approval. If they never saw him in action, they would never fully understand his passion for chocolate. Theodor was sure that his father would approve of this chosen path in life if only he could drop the notion of Theodor following in his judicial footsteps, though that eventuality was unlikely. Luckily, his mother would approve of just about anything so long as he was successful and had a beautiful woman on his arm.

Getting the woman wasn't the challenge, keeping her was, and the woman he wanted didn't seem to want anything but to win her little prize. He, on the other hand, was uninterested in seeking out anyone else. From the moment she had played with him on the train, he knew she was someone he wanted to be in his life. If it weren't for the lure of the grant money making her behave in such a devious manner, he suspected they would be sharing a third or even fourth date by now.

Across the street, a steady stream of workers carrying furniture and boxes came in and out of the creamery. Holly was likely making her ice-creams now, as he was making his chocolates. He didn't know much about her craft, and she probably didn't know much about his, but learning each other's profession could make for an interesting date, if they ever stopped being enemies.

He lamented that their burgeoning relationship had been tainted by competition. He knew he could forgive her ambition at his expense, but he didn't know whether she could ever lower the walls she had erected around her heart long before he met her. For a couple of brief moments, he had seen through the cracks in her defenses. The question pin-balling in his mind was if he had enough energy to keep trying, to wait for her to knock her bulwarks down. That time might come someday, but not yet.

While she was over there formulating her victory, he was preparing for his own. He had roasted his beans to perfection, created the base chocolate, unsweetened, raw, and ready to be worked into lovely products. Fresh ingredients were a must, though some things like the candied orange peel and raspberry filling had to be made earlier in the week, he sourced what he could locally until he had time to create his own specialty additions.

Theodor selected his moulds and prepared the layers of each variety he planned to offer at his tasting. It was important to have a good showing, since gourmet chocolates are somewhat of an expensive delicacy, and he hoped to change occasional foot traffic to a more everyday pleasure the same way folks spend eight dollars on a ten-cent cup of coffee without batting an eye.

First impressions were everything, and he had received plenty of positive feedback at the open house with a lot of interest coming his way. It helped that Alfonso was there acting like a personal hype-man and got the guests to sample the selections he brought.

While the chocolate was setting up, Theodor prepared for his event on the sidewalk outside. He started with the shade-tents and tables. Like a street market, he created unique stations where people could experience different sides of his business. The tasting table featured samples. The second area was for beverages: sparkling and fruit infused water. But he was most excited for the last area where he would show his skills and artistry with some quick tips and a display of how he creates his sweets.

While taping a paper cloth to the underside of one of his folding tables, Holly skipped down her side of the street and stole his attention. It was hard to miss her in a white sundress. A yellow bow at the back of her head bounced with each step and teased his imagination. He caught her gaze for a split second before she turned her face to the activity outside her own shop.

He stood. "What the heck is she up to?" he said to no one. His tents weren't the only ones going up. Two shade structures jutted out from her front windows and out into the road, covering the parking spots. His hands went to his hips as he watched men setting up bistro tables and chairs in the shade. Another crew ran cables and extension cords to the other shaded area.

Whatever her aim, he suspected subterfuge. She entered her front door and looked over her shoulder at him with a smirk and a wave of her fingers.

"Blake Holly Hollis," he shouted and marched across the street, dodging a woman bumbling along the cobblestones on her bike. "What are you doing?"

"Enjoying this beautiful weather," she said with a shimmy. "What are you doing? Here to spy on my shop?"

Since she accused, he took the chance to look around. It was as though he was in a secret garden, just like she had told him she wanted her shop to look. "You knew I was having my tasting event today. So, what are you doing out here?"

"What, like two shops can't hold events on the same day? I got my event approved over a week ago, did you?" Holly said and he wanted to wipe the smug grin off her face.

"Of course, I did. That's not the point. I don't think you understand, I need today to be successful."

"Why can't we both have a successful event today? People come for my ice cream, and see your chocolates, and vice versa. It's a win-win. I thought this would be a good thing."

"It's a Holly show, and you know it."

"Listen, Teddy, as much as I would love to stand here and listen to you, I have a lot of work to do to prepare for today. I mean you no harm." She crossed her finger over her heart. "I swear it."

Stunned silence was a real thing, though he hadn't exactly experienced the feeling to this extent before, he truly was locked in place. How could he trust what she was saying after everything that happened? Was she still being mischievous or really playing nice? He honestly didn't know, and he didn't have time to figure it out now. "I hope you're telling the truth. But know that bridges, once burned down, won't be rebuilt easily." He forced his feet to move away from her before sounding even more pathetic. "I hope you do well today."

"Believe it or not. I hope you succeed too. But I still need those fifty-thousand dollars, and I'm willing to do what it takes to get it." She placed a hand on his forearm and turned his face to hers. "This is how it has to be."

He understood her just fine. At least he knew the sentiment she was attempting to express. The difference between their individual desires to win was the line he was unwilling to cross. Her line was decidedly located elsewhere, though he wasn't certain of the precise location. As he made his way back across the street to his shop, he wondered whether her ability to push the limits would be enough to propel her to success.

Time would tell if his efforts would lead to success. For now, he had a few final touches to add to his event set-up. A white van pulled up next to his shop and the side door slid open. Gold and white balloons poured out and floated skyward as far as their tethers would permit. The delivery driver placed the weighted bag on the ground and closed the slider.

Behind the van, a small semi-truck stopped and obscured the creamery from his view. Ignoring whatever she had going on, Theodor thanked the driver and began securing the balloons to the supports of the shade tents. Playing off Holly's choice of spray paint, the gold balloons shimmered in the sun and would help draw attention to his location. Assisting with the flow of traffic, he positioned the groups of balloons to help guide people from one activity to the next.

With the final bunch attached, he stood back and clapped his hands, pleased with the way his event appeared. "Today is going to be a good day."

As the truck separating him from Holly pulled away, he realized he may have spoken too soon. A gigantic green and pink balloon arch spanned the street. Behind the arch and half-way down the block, workers lowered the side panels of a shipping container, revealing a folded carnival ride, like they were opening a pop-up book. Buckets hung from a steel structure that went up in minutes. Two guys climbed a central ladder and bolted two ends of an octagon together at the top.

"A Ferris wheel?" Theodor let his bun down for the sole purpose of ripping his hair out. "You've got to be kidding me! I wonder how much that cost!" He threw his hands in the air and kicked an empty bucket through his store's open front door.

There was nothing he could do to compete with her resources, which begged the question: if she had all this money, plenty enough to rent a Ferris wheel, then why did she need the grant money at all? There was one way he would find out. And he intended to.

Slapping a set of balloons from his way that were blowing in the breeze, he stepped towards the street, stopping short of the curb. Across the road, a band was setting up equipment and doing a sound check in the spot where the workers had been laying cables. She had it all, and he needed something big if he was going to compete. He needed something fast.

Theodor snapped his fingers as his mind searched for an answer. For a man who always had a strategy, he wondered why everything he was doing was falling short? He snapped his fingers at his realization. He was failing at the game, because he was playing by someone else's rules. It was high time he got off his heels and got onto offense.

He took his phone out and rang Alfonso. "Hey bro. I need a favor. Do you think you can bring the guests to my shop for let's say, a field trip? In one hour."

CHAPTER 17

FROM ALL APPEARANCES, TEDDY'S CHOCOLATE TASTING HAD BEEN A success. Holly had watched the crowds of people gathering to try his products and showing interest in his culinary demonstration. If she hadn't been so busy managing her own event, she might have given into her curiosity and attended his instead.

With most of the ice cream samples gone or melted, and her crew tearing down the tents, a very serious looking Teddy was marching straight toward her. "Come with me," he demanded and took her hand before she could respond. She felt like a petulant child about to be punished, but they were heading for the Ferris wheel which didn't frighten her so much.

She tugged on Teddy's grip, but he only held her tighter. "What are you doing?"

"Hush," he said without making eye contact and approached the ride's operator. Handing him an undisclosed amount of folded bills, Teddy gestured for her to get into the seat. He followed next and sat beside her on the narrow bucket. There was no extra room. Her hip pressed against his and their knees touched. The operator secured the metal bar across their laps and activated the mechanics, sending them rocking skyward.

It wasn't long before they neared the apex of the wheel, and the ride stopped. Their bucket swung forward and backward at the jerk. Below, Millie and Alfonso got into another bucket and the ride started again. The view was amazing from up so high. Holly was glad to not be afraid of heights, though her fingers clasped the cross-bar with all her might for fear of what was on the tip of Teddy's tongue.

Teddy placed his hand on her knee, likely sensing her tension. But she wasn't tense because of the ride, she was tense because of his presence and proximity. Her body steeled in an effort to deny anyone entry into her inner self. The ride stopped again, and they dangled high above the lights strung across Main.

"I apologize for the theatrics, but I knew you wouldn't come with me willingly."

She was about to protest but knew he was correct. "Alright. You got me all to yourself, what now?" Her heart pounded behind the lace bodice of her sundress. If this encounter was like their others, it would be passion fueled chaos; a messed-up emotion she was becoming accustomed to craving.

"It's about time we got some things straightened out."

She could tell by his flat tone that he was serious. She twisted in her seat so that she was open to him. Notwithstanding her struggle to keep him out, she hoped he would be the person to triumphantly tear down her walls for good, but the knot in her gut told her to run. He was smart because she had nowhere to flee to. "I don't really have a choice, do I?"

"Holly," he brushed her curtain bangs behind her ear with his warm fingers and she caught a whiff of cocoa on the breeze. "Why are you so determined to win, when you obviously have everything that you need. I mean, who rents a Ferris wheel?" he chuckled though the sound was tight in his throat. "Who does that?"

She didn't want him to know the truth. Her mother had cut her off unless she agreed to 'leave this whole creamery business behind her'. "I don't know why it was so much easier to talk to you before," she said remembering their time on the train. "Before you were my competition, that is. I can't see past it."

"Don't you see that we're not adversaries? We could have put on an event today together and found much more success that way. I'm not talking about sharing resources or workers or anything else, but I am talking about not trying to sabotage the other. I spent all afternoon plotting a way to get back at you, and do you know what I came up with?"

She shook her head, afraid to know what his next move was going to be. She swallowed the lump of guilt down her throat.

"Nothing. I came up empty," he said, and she swore there was a glimmer of a tear behind his dark eyes. "And do you know why?"

"Because you're a good person and I'm a spoiled brat who gets whatever she wants." Her frank answer surprised her.

"Yes." Teddy shook his head ever so slightly like her response surprised him too. "Only, I think you're not getting what you really want."

"And what do you think I want?" *Please say you.*

"You want the same thing I do," Teddy said.

Please say you want to be with me too.

"You want to be valued and respected. You want to impress your family who think you aren't making the right choices in life, and you want someone to love you for who you really are."

He was good. And correct. "But how—"

He placed a finger over her lips. "I'm not done. The problem you're facing is that your parents want different things for you and making one of them happy means upsetting the other. And as for finding someone to love the real you, that'll never happen so long as you hide from everyone with your perfect hair and pretty teeth, practiced manners and deviant behavior."

She opened her mouth to speak but no words came out. It dawned on her like a ray of morning sunlight that he could only know her intimate fears because he recognized his own truths and struggles in her. Sadness overwhelmed her and moistened her eyes as she recalled what he had told her during their first meeting. He was trying to prove himself to people who didn't care to see him walk his own way in life. They really were two peas in a pod.

"I don't know how to be anything other than this." She pointed to herself and swept the back of her hands down her body.

"So why do you want that grant money so much, enough to do what you're doing to me?"

"Truth?"

He rocked his chin up once indicating for her to continue.

"At first, I was afraid if my creamery isn't a success I'll have nothing else but to go work for my mother on the farm. Spending time on a failed venture means I'll have missed out on other opportunities. I was hoping to win the money and shut them up," she said and shifted her eyes away.

"And now?" he said and moved his face in front of hers.

"My mother cut me off the day before we got arrested. Everything you saw today; I had prepaid for, or else I would have had no event. So, I need to win the money. There, now you know."

Teddy nodded. "Millie told me at the station, actually, but I knew that wasn't the whole story. Now you're telling me you need the money to prove why you don't need your parents' money?"

"Are you mocking me?" she said and recoiled from him as far as she could in the small seat.

"Are you two love-birds gonna kiss yet, or what?" Millie hollered from a bucket behind her.

Holly had forgotten they weren't completely alone and twisted around to see Millie. "Why don't you mind your own business. And if you want some action, then get it from Alfonso."

Alfonso grinned at the suggestion as Holly turned back to Teddy.

"Holly, I'm not making fun of your situation. But I think it would be fair if you knew mine before taking another turn against me."

If she didn't feel bad a minute ago, she did now. She hadn't considered him, not even once while plotting his demise. "Tell me then."

"Your little stunt in the forest that got us arrested ... It was the final straw with my dad. He got the charges dropped and promptly canceled my credit cards. I was already on thin ice with him, but now ..." he paused again, and she held his hands on his lap. "I am utterly alone."

"Teddy, no."

"All I have is this shop and this little town that barely knows me." Teddy pulled his slumped shoulders back. "You've worked very hard at winning at my expense and it's made it difficult for me to gain the trust of the people of Christmas Cove. And I'm tired of playing cat and mouse with you."

"More like Mouse Trap," she said and giggled, knowing the pranks she had played on him. "I still want to win the money. Is that wrong?"

"I don't blame you for wanting what you want. That part I actually fully understand."

"So, what is it that you want from me? A truce ... A real one?" Holly allowed her body to relax into the bucket for the first time since boarding. "Because I still want to win, and there's more at stake for me now."

"Blake Holly Hollis, I want you to win if it means so much to you. All I ask is that you leave me out of it. You win by being the absolute best joint in town. Fair and square."

"What if I don't want to leave you be. What if I want something else." She leaned into him wanting him to kiss away the torment she felt inside at having treated him so poorly. "What if I start to show you the real me like you were talking about?"

Teddy's hand slid up her arm to the nape of her neck and he held her in place. His dark eyes searched hers for truth, while she hoped he was picking up the apology behind them. "No more pretending with me."

She nodded her head, and his lips crushed against hers, taking her with his mouth. His aura encompassed them both and created a bubble of time and space around their bodies. Heat crept over her skin at his touch. His fingers encircled her waist on one side while his others played in her hair at the back of her head.

With no room to do much else in the small bucket, she closed the space between them. His heart pounded against her chest. Each thump was like a little secret passing between them and soon there would be nothing stopping her from falling for Theodor Black.

They jolted forward, the operator down below engaging the ride again, and caused their bucket to swing. Clapping vibrated off the metal structure from Millie and Alfonso, and all Holly could do was shut her eyes and cringe at having had an audience for such a vulnerable moment. Teddy sat straight in his seat but held her hand as the ride came back down.

The operator stopped their swinging and unlatched the safety bar. "Ten minutes," he said. "I hope you got what you needed."

Teddy patted the man on his shoulder and gave a grinning nod.

Heading back to her shop, the musicians had gone, and the remnants of the melted ice cream dripped onto the sidewalk below the tables. "I'll help you finish cleaning up if you help me?" he asked.

"Since we're both poor now? That sounds like a good plan."

CHAPTER 18

FOR THE FIRST TIME ALL SUMMER, AND IN LONGER THAN SHE COULD remember, Holly took a Monday off. She had been working nonstop at creating her dream ice cream shop, and all the pieces were coming together nicely. Now, with only a few items to complete —a working bathroom was a must and she still needed to hire the rest of the staff—her mind was finally in a place where she could take a day to rest.

Her free-sample event on Saturday had been a wild success aided by the foot traffic from Teddy's chocolate tasting. Of course he had been irritated, thinking she was just trying to outdo him, but the huge balloon display over the street and the Ferris wheel had helped draw more attention to the area for them both.

Out on the lawn bordering the cove's shoreline, Holly lay back against her folding lounge chair. A light breeze fluttered the scalloped edges of her beach umbrella positioned between her chair and Millie's. Through cracked eyelids, she watched children splash at the water's edge. The moving air cooled her skin from the midday heat, but the water was looking more and more enticing with each passing minute.

"So, what happened next?" Millie asked. "We could see you two, but I couldn't hear what you were talking about."

A smile creeped across Holly's face, and she was sure her flush was caused by the memory of the way Teddy held her and kissed her and not from the sun beating down around her. "All I can say is that we came to an … agreement."

"Is that what you call that kiss?" Millie laughed. "We couldn't hear you, but we saw it all." Millie fanned herself with her hand.

There was nothing that could cause her to forget about the steamy exchange any time soon, but Holly fiddled with her messy bun on the top of her head to try. "It turns out that we're both dealing with parents who don't support us. Teddy just wants to make a life for himself. And for whatever reason, I keep trying to prove something to my mother when I know exactly what she wants; to go into the business with her."

"As sad as that is. At least you know now, and you don't have to keep trying with her," Millie said and adjusted the rim of her bucket hat. "Alfonso mentioned that Teddy's dad canceled his credit cards after the arrest."

"You knew and didn't say?" Holly wasn't surprised that it hadn't come up. She knew she hadn't given Millie much chance to get a word in between her venting about Teddy and laying floors. "I wish I hadn't been so selfish."

"Because you feel terrible for how you treated him?"

"Of course I do. But what's worse is I still wonder if he's got something up his sleeve. Like his whole let's-be-honest, nice-guy act last night was just that." Her suspicions were probably projection, because before last night, it was she who would have done something so underhanded while he had really been a saint about the whole thing.

"Holly, do you really think he's capable? The guy that plays with chocolate all day and smiles every time he sees you?" Millie had a point.

"You're not wrong. I don't know. You know why I have trust issues."

"Typical rich girl problems. You all go to the Med and get cheated on by a loser boyfriend, move home, and hit the restart button on a fresh life."

Holly slid her sunglasses up to her head and twisted in her chair to look Millie in the eyes. She needed to see her face. "Yes, actually. You don't know what it's like to have every friend, every teacher, my tennis coach, my last boyfriend, like all kinds of people using me to win favors with my parents. I'm tired of being someone's second choice."

"I hear you, but play this out. What would Teddy gain from being associated with you? What's his ulterior motive?" Millie said and removed her own glasses revealing her raised eyebrow. "From what I can see, you have nothing to lose by letting that hot man into your life."

Holly adjusted the red fabric of her triangle bikini top and returned her sunglasses to shield her eyes. She laid back and soaked in the sun hitting her lower half while she let Millie's words sink in. Was it time for her to trust someone? And if the answer was yes, why not Teddy?

Her skin sizzled and moisture beaded up on her stomach. Seeing as she had chosen to take a day off on what was the hottest day of the year so far, she intended to squeeze every ounce of vitamin D from the day that she could. Holly dug in her cooler bag for a can of sparkling water and cracked the metal tab on the top. The crisp sound was refreshing on its own, but the taste of sparkling coconut water was even better.

"How do you feel about piña colada sorbet?" she asked and took another sip.

"You're thinking about adding it to the menu?" Millie said and took the can from Holly's hand. She sipped the water and handed it back. "It could be good."

Holly grabbed another drink from the cooler and handed it to

Millie. "If I had a dollar for every time I was burned by someone, I wouldn't need the grant money."

"You don't really need it. You just wanted to win." Millie cracked open her drink and the fizz sprayed onto Holly's legs. "Sorry," she said while Holly rubbed the flavored water into her skin. "What I mean is that you have everything you need to start your business and you're just looking for some street cred. I don't blame you for being competitive, but don't gaslight yourself into thinking you need it."

"How are you so wise?"

Millie tittered. "I am not wise. I have that thing where I always think I'm too much for people. It's taught me to read situations well since I don't read people well."

"It's called ADHD." With a laugh, Holly held up her can. "Cheers, to two friends blazing our own paths." They clanked their cans together just as a water bomb crashed into their hands from the side.

The moment Holly had waited all day for had finally come. "WATER BALLOON FIGHT!" she yelled.

Between their chairs, she uncovered a bucket filled to the brim with water balloons. After the Ferris wheel situation, Alfonso tipped off Millie to the men's impending attack. Millie told Holly. And Holly recruited some of her new friends to fight in the most epic clash of their lives. She grabbed two balloons and tossed them in the direction where the first one had come from. It hit the ground about twenty feet away and threw up a cloud of water droplets.

"Take the flank!" Millie shouted and pointed to a pre-positioned stack of chairs.

Holly loaded the crook of her left arm with as many balloons as she could carry and took off towards cover. Once in position and holding enough ammo to get a couple good hits in, she cried out, "NOW!" and a dozen children ran into the combat zone. Some bigger kids carried buckets filled with balloons while others lined up in the middle of the lawn.

In front of the children and teens, Teddy, Leo, Alfonso, and two other guys who she didn't recognize prepared to face off with their own cache of water balloons.

Thandie, who Holly had met at America's house for girl's night, joined Holly behind the chairs. "This'll be fun. I've been wanting to get back at Grant, the tall guy with his hat on backwards. He's mine."

The whole silly affair had the women giddy. "I haven't had a water balloon fight since I was a little girl. Well, it wasn't really a fight as much as it was me and Millie ganging up on one of the poor stable hands. I don't know why this feels so good."

Across the lawn, Millie gave the final order. "Attack at will!"

Holly and Thandie went straight for the two tallest guys, Teddy and Grant. Tossing one balloon after the other, they progressed their position with each explosion. Teddy ducked and dodged almost all of her balloons, but her last one hit him square in his chest. His hands covered his heart like he had been wounded, and the water caused his white cotton tee to appear translucent. She stopped, knowing she was in trouble. His head slumped down, but his eyes locked onto hers like a lion stalking prey. He snarled and ripped his wet shirt in half, discarding it onto the grass.

Standing broad and glistening in the sunlight, his toned chest and abs caught the shadows in all the right places. It was getting hot out there in more than one way. With her last ammo, she pointed at him and wiggled her pointer finger to call him over to her.

Teddy smirked at her invitation with a fire blazing in his eyes. He sprinted to her, closing the distance in only a few steps and allowed her no time to retreat. Not slowing down, his arm crashed into her midriff, and he lifted her off the ground like a line-backer making a tackle. The momentum had her swinging all the way around his body where he caught her against his chest once she made a full rotation.

"Hi," he said and pecked her on the mouth.

With her arms around his neck, she matched his smirk. "Two points for me, none for you."

"You only hit me once."

"Maybe so," she said as she squeezed her remaining ammo in her grasp, digging her nails into the thin rubber until the water balloon splashed over his head. "Two points."

"We're playing like that, huh?" He put her down near a row of baskets filled with outdoor toys. Teddy reached into one of the bins and came out holding a rather large water blaster the length of his arm.

"Teddy, no. Don't you dare," she said and was already running away. A steady stream of water hit her backside and sprayed outward, wetting her all over. "Theodor Black! You're going to get it!"

He kept his distance behind her, probably for ideal viewing and soaking range. "Is that a promise?"

"You're flirting right now?" she said and ducked behind a beach umbrella sitting low in the ground. "This isn't a date, Teddy. This is war!" Balloons and water flew through the air above her, but there was more laughter than she'd heard in a long time. Holly really did love to laugh, and it had been too long since her stomach hurt from joy.

In the shade of the umbrella, someone had put a load of water balloons. She took one in each hand and tossed them one at a time in his direction. She heard them splash onto the grass, not his sculpted body. Needing a quick peek, she peered around the edge of the umbrella, but he wasn't there. Across the lawn, Millie chased Alfonso with an open hose, and Thandie and her man were busy soaking each other with blasters. Children were running and jumping in newly formed puddles while others jumped off the end of the dock into the lake.

"Where are you, Teddy?" she searched all the spots where he might hide.

"Surprise," he said from behind her.

Twisting to see him, she put her hands up in surrender as he doused her with whatever water remained in his blaster. "I give. I give." She smiled while wiping water from her face.

"It's not that easy." He dropped his emptied blaster and fell to his knees in front of her.

Walking his hands out in front of him, he urged her to lay back in the soft green grass. His bare chest hovered inches above her bikini clad body. Her breath caught in her throat at his proximity. She wasn't frightened, she was intrigued, and the tipped over umbrella gave them privacy to play.

"What do you want?" she said more breathlessly than she had wanted, but her desire for him overwhelmed her senses. Her heart drummed against her ribs and her pulse vibrated in her stomach. She wanted to stay in control, but she surrendered to him anyway. She craved his lips to be on hers, but she wouldn't dare say it. She wanted him to be the one to declare his desire.

Reaching up, she removed his hair elastic. His shoulder length hair cascaded around his face and caused him to look more dangerous than he had before. The light filtered through the umbrella, casting a red glow in his eyes and shading his already dark stubble. He grinned, knowing what he was doing to her, and for a moment, she liked the freedom in being so wild.

He walked his hands forward; his hip bones grazed her inner thighs as he moved up her body until she was resting flat on her back and his face matched hers. The tip of his nose brushed back and forth on hers, and his lips glistened with moisture.

Holly was helpless to look anywhere else, pleading with him to satisfy her need to be touched by him.

"I like you in red," he said into her ear and backed off without a single kiss, leaving her frustrated and wanting more. He stood and someone she couldn't see but could hear with an Italian accent tossed a filled blaster into Teddy's hands. "I'll give you ten seconds."

"One." She counted for herself, knowing he wasn't bluffing and stood. "Two." She teased her hands up his stomach and chest. "Three." She paused and closed her eyes. "Four." She peeked up and saw him close his eyes too. She kissed his lips and stole the gun right out of his hands. "Five. You better get going," she said and moved away from him. "Six."

"Alright, I give up. Just do it already." It was Teddy's turn to put his hands up in surrender. She took full advantage of having him to herself, drenching him with the water and soaking every inch of his body and pink swim trunks.

With the blaster cleared of contents, she dropped it and ran toward the dock, screaming the whole way as he chased her into the water. She soared off the end of the dock and he followed her right in, landing a foot away from her. His hands reached out for her waist and pulled her in before she could get her bearings.

They bobbed together in the refreshing water. Her arms wrapped around his neck as he encircled her waist with his strong hands. Their bodies pressed together below the waterline. Her toes barely touched the smooth pebbles beneath her, but Teddy carried most of her weight.

"Come to the firefly parade with me tonight?" he said low.

"Like a date?"

"Like, my date."

She liked how possessive he was, like she was the only creature in the world he craved, and she was starting to thirst for him too. Her kiss was her answer, and she was very agreeable.

CHAPTER 19

THE MAN IN THE MIRROR'S REFLECTION LOOKED CALM AND COOL IN his creamy linen shirt and pants, but Theodor's blood was swarming red-hot with anticipation in his veins. He washed his hands in the sink and pressed cold water into the skin on his cheeks. Resting his hand on the sides of the sink bowl, he locked eyes with himself. "It's just a date. You can do this."

Show time, he thought and ran his fingers through his loose hair. He had coiled it into an easy knot at first, but Holly seemed to prefer his hair down, so he changed his mind and his style. Because his father hated Theodor's long hair, he was accustomed to slicking it back whenever he had worked at the firm. Here, in Christmas Cove, there was nothing holding him to anyone else's standards anymore. If he wished to wear his hair loose, he would.

A soft knocking came at his cabin door, and he said goodbye to the reflection in the bathroom mirror. Outside, Holly waited. A single pane of glass and the sheer curtain separated him from his date. The silhouette teased him. She was obviously wearing nothing since her every curve was visible in the shadow.

Opening the door, he now understood why her shape had appeared naked. She wore a red, skin-tight dress that hugged her beautiful body and left little to his overactive imagination. The square neckline suited her well, and the long hemline stopped just below her knees. His hands covered his heart. "You're so lovely, it hurts."

She smiled and kicked one foot up towards her bottom and highlighted her gold, sparkly flat sandals. "Thanks. I thought you might like this dress."

He nodded, unable to form a sentence that would sound gentlemanly. He liked the dress very much, but his mind was busy imagining what it would look like in a pile on the floor of his cabin instead of stretched across her skin. He presented his hand to her, and he pulled the door shut behind him with his other. "Have you ever been to a firefly parade before?"

"No. I think this is a new thing since the Foundry opened last year," she said as they began to walk towards the Foundry's main structure, Harbour House. The packed gravel pathway, lined with little solar lanterns, made the short trip up the hill an easy one, though neither of them was in a hurry with all the scuffing heels against the ground. "I never had anything like this in the city. Too much light for fireflies."

"When I was little, Millie and I would stay in the pasture after the horses had gone in for the evening. If you stood really still in the long grass, lightning bugs would hover right in front of your face. I swore they were little fairies put there to sprinkle magic on the world."

"I like that," he said and threaded his fingers through hers. Dusk was settling into darkness and the fireflies were already dancing around the property. "I have no thoughts about fireflies, none as nice as yours anyway. I figured it was an Ohio thing. Like something that normal people have in middle-America. Come to find out, my whole life, I was only a couple hours train ride away from experiencing them for myself. Manhattan is great, but it's like living in a bubble sometimes."

"I get what you mean. You can be so close to something and

not even see it, not even know it's there to be seen." Holly nudged his arm with her elbow which he took to mean she was seeing him in a new way.

Being in her presence felt so natural at some times, and like torture at others. He considered the double meaning of what she had just said. Was he too close to see what was really happening between them? Was she? He nudged her back as they came to the front of the barn-like building.

Outside the Harbour House, the activities director, Thandie, handed out lanterns no bigger than a coffee mug, along with bug-catching kits; a medium-sized mason jar and a net. Beside the path, there was a table with baskets filled with individual snack packs of little sandwiches, fruit, and cheese, a choice of either water or a split of something bubbly.

Releasing Holly's hand, Theodor took the basket and added two little champagne bottles. In his free hand, he held the lantern allowing her to have the mason jar and net. Other guests had already begun their parade. Theodor and Holly followed behind the group in front of them, giving themselves enough space to speak without being overheard by other folks.

Plunged into darkness within a minute, they entered a section of the property where newly planted trees lined the route and lush green and white ground-cover spilled over the edges of a gravel path. The lantern was just enough to illuminate their feet without interfering with their ability to see the lightning bugs springing up from the ground.

Holly pointed at every firefly she saw, her excitement seemingly growing with each passing second. He could have watched her hips sway back and forth all night. Better than that, he could watch her lips curl up at the sides and brighten her eyes forever. "You know, you're pretty fun to be around when you're not trying to destroy me."

"Well, right now, I'm too busy concentrating on catching a fairy to be bothered with scheming of any other kind." She turned and he held the lantern to her flushed face. She bit her smiling lower lip between her teeth and her eyes were wide with joy. "I could go back to tormenting you if you'd like, but the pixies won't wait."

Little did she know that her mere existence was torment enough. "That won't be necessary," he said. "I do want you to get your prize before they all go to bed tonight though. Should we go up a little further?"

They paraded up the trail until it turned back down towards the lake where a large gazebo glowed in the half-moonlight. Several guests stood under the gazebo roof while others sat in the lawn area enjoying their snacks.

"Let's stay on the path for now, see where it goes. This area is busy." As he spoke, a child ran between them, flinging his net through the air. If he was chasing a bug at all, it certainly wasn't a firefly, as there were none near them, but the kid's enthusiasm elicited a giggle from Holly.

"I think that's a good idea," she said with the laughter still present in her words.

Around the next bend, there was a fork in the path, one way hugged the shoreline, and the other meandered up a low hill between two cabins. She veered towards the less traveled, up-hill route, and he was happy to follow her. Just ahead, dozens of fireflies hovered about the grass, floating skyward and falling back down. The little bugs blazed in spurts of electricity that matched the little sparks he had been experiencing throughout his own body since earlier that afternoon.

He chuckled in his throat, remembering how she looked wearing her tiny red bikini—as delicious as a fresh cherry—and running away from him while he soaked her through. It was his privilege to witness her now, so full of bliss, knowing he much preferred being her friend to being her enemy. This was fun.

He set down his basket and watched her move through the

grass on the hunt for her prey. "I have faith in you, Blake Holly Hollis."

"Shh. I'm hunting wabbits," she said with far too serious a tone than the moment called for and stalked a flickering bug about two feet in front of her.

Her lantern lay on its side in the grass behind her feet and illuminated her backside. He was in no hurry to miss this view. Theodor shoved his hands in his pockets and stood comfortably, observing her fling her net through the air.

"Shoot! I missed that one," she said as she twirled all the way around, unaware of the show she was putting on for him.

"Keep going, honey," he said, and she looked over her shoulder at him with her brow raised. It was a term of endearment, and though it had come out naturally, it sounded sexier than the alternative, 'babe' or 'darling'. *No regrets.*

She stalked another firefly and swung her net again. This time it made a swooshing sound, followed by a squeal from her pretty mouth. He could do nothing but enjoy the entertainment. She was pure perfection, content in her childlike delight at having won her prize.

"Bring me the jar, quick," she whisper-yelled.

"Why are we whispering?" he said and opened the jar lid.

She held the net upside down over the rim. "I don't want to scare it," she said, still whispering, and dropped the firefly into the glass container.

Theodor secured the lid and switched the net in her grasp for the jar. Her soft fingers brushed against his in the transfer, and he wondered if she was tempting him on purpose now. "I think you already scared it when you took it captive."

"Oh, hush. It's just a bug." She held the container at eye level between their faces. "And look how cute it is." She was smitten.

They watched the light flicker on and off for a minute, mesmerized by the chemistry of it. He wished he knew something interesting about fireflies, instead of puffins, and could impress her with his knowledge, but he didn't. So, he settled on flattery instead. "I think it's cute, but I think you're cuter."

"Cuter, huh?" she said without taking her eyes off the jar. As the bug lit up, so did her face.

"Captivating?" he added.

She caught his eye through the jar. "Better."

"Enchanting? Bewitching?" He pushed the jar away. He was so close; he could practically taste her vanilla lip balm. "And so very sexy."

"You just like my dress." She accused in a whisper, her words hardly making it past her lips.

He brushed his thumb across her pillowy soft lips "It's more than that. Your confidence is infectious. You find pleasure when you stop caring about what others think—"

"Teddy, I'm only that way around you. And it's the most frustrating thing ever."

There was a cry in her voice that he wanted to take away if he could know where it stemmed from. Maybe someday, he would find out and make all the hurt disappear into the past where it belonged. He pushed her hair behind her ear and let her continue.

"You pierce my walls every time you look at me like that. Every time you make me laugh, even when I'm being awful to you." She giggled. "Even sitting in prison."

He wanted to kiss her, to possess her mouth with his and make her forget about the weight of the world she was carrying. The day had been as ideal as any day he had ever had, and he was afraid it was too good to be true. The woman standing before him was the same person who had nearly ruined his business, or at least she had tried with all her stunts and pranks.

He couldn't hear anymore. Not now. Not when he needed to process what she had just admitted to. She was right that she was different when she was around him, but it was yet to be seen if that would prove to be a good or bad thing. He stepped back far enough to stop feeling the heat from her body. "We should head back soon. Do you want to sit on the dock and enjoy our snack first?"

Holly nodded and picked her net up from the ground. She hugged her jar into her chest as they made their way down the path along the shore. As they walked, he did his best to ignore his ever more conflicting doubts about her. His suspicions were like little demons trampling on his future. He just needed more time to know if she was being real with him, and time would tell if he would be able to fully open up to her.

The gravel path gave way to the worn wooden boards of the dock. Theodor removed his shoes and placed them just off to the side. "May I?" he asked and fell to his knees beside Holly. She lifted one foot, and he slid the strap over the back of her heel. Her slender ankle fit in his palm as though she was made for him to touch. He slid the sandal from her foot, letting his fingers glide up the inside of her calf before repeating the process on the other side.

Barefoot, they sat on the edge of the dock and let their feet dangle over the side. The water was just at his toes, and he kicked his legs back and forth. The water gently splashed underneath like rain dripping into a puddle.

He cracked open the champagne splits and handed her one. "No glasses," he said and let the cool bubbles tickle his tongue.

"Teddy?" she said as he began to speak too. "You go ahead."

"No, you. I insist," he said and took a sip from the bottle.

"Today has been ..."

"Pretty great?"

"Yeah," she said and tucked her long blonde hair behind her ear on the side closest to him. She was nervous, he could see it in the tension of her long neck and the quick rising and falling of her chest.

"You're thinking it's too good to be true?" he asked, because that's what he was thinking too.

She nodded. "I want you to meet my parents." She took a long swig from her bottle.

"This is moving fast," he teased.

"Not like that." She rocked him with her shoulder. "I want you to meet them so you can understand me better. I am sorry for treating you so badly the last couple weeks and I think it would help if you saw the whole picture."

"I think the thing that scares you the most is that I do understand you. It's the only reason I could be so patient with you while you were trying to take me down. I knew since we met on the train that there was far more to learn about Blake Holly Hollis." Theodor took a deep breath and another swig. "I appreciate your apology."

"There's an exhibition at the farm tomorrow morning. I need to make an appearance anyway and maybe smooth things over with my mother, if she's in a good mood. It's not far from here. Do you think you can come with me?"

He really wanted to. "I can't. I have a delivery at the shop that I have to be there for. I have a ton of work to do still. Your shop is way further along than mine, and—"

"It's fine. It was a silly thing to ask."

Theodor caught her chin in his hand and turned her face towards him. "It's not silly. I just can't tomorrow." He looked out at the lake water shimmering under the stars. "How about I make it up to you with a moonlit boat ride tomorrow evening. Eight o'clock?"

She licked her lips and signaled her agreement with a blink. He let his lips do the talking and caressed the spot where her tongue had just been. She was far too delicious for his own taste, and for his own good. He had a whole day to plan their next date, and it would be a good one!

CHAPTER 20

THERE WAS LITTLE ELSE HOLLY DISLIKED MORE THAN SHOWING UP to an event alone. The occasion was irrelevant because the situation would play out the same each time. She would walk inside, her mother would thrust any number of eligible members of the club at her, and she would make nice to get along. Holly's mother was fixated on maintaining appearances, while Holly was split between keeping the peace with her mother and being herself for her father.

Having parked at the end of a very long line of luxury cars skirting the semi-circular drive, Holly walked towards a sprawling clubhouse. The farm's compound accommodated meeting spaces and all the offices for the trainers, partners, and executives who all worked tirelessly to be the masters of the horse racing community. All she saw was wasted money, though she would rightly admit to being a beneficiary of her mother's success.

If the horses were the main draw, the clubhouse was next. Holly had always loved the style of the building. When Holly was a little girl, the club had undergone an extensive renovation and was remodeled in the Victorian style. The single-story structure was painted white with black accents which allowed the copper downspouts and exterior lighting to shine.

Tall, rounded peaks accentuated the roofline and reminded her of a castle. Even though the towers were decorative in nature, as children, she and Millie had gained access to one and set up the space as their own personal girl fort. She looked up to the roofline and wondered which one still held the treasures they had stored there.

As she approached the front doors, Holly caught a whiff of the honeysuckle bushes that hugged the foundation. Her mother's favorite color had always been yellow, and mounds of golden flowers spilled out from below the bushes and onto the border of the drive. Catching her reflection in the glass panel as a valet opened the front door, she realized she unintentionally had worn a yellow dress that day. No doubt her mother would assume the choice was an effort to pander.

"Good day, Miss Hollis," the valet said as she entered, and she flashed a smile.

At some point, she was unsure when exactly, the staff had stopped calling her Miss Blake or Lady Blake and started calling her by her surname. It made her feel older than she thought herself to be, but it also made her feel more important than she was too. Her mother was Mrs. Hollis. Her father was Mister Hollis. Her parents had worked hard to get where they were now, but she was just there; the girl with the good fortune to have been born to successful parents.

Upon entering and following the line of the green and yellow carpet runner, she spotted her mother right away. It was hard to miss the tall, slender woman, with blonde hair styled higher than heaven, and a smile to match. Her white fascinator was tilted to one side and hid her eyes from Holly's view, though she must have sensed Holly's presence in the room with a straightening of her spine. Her laughter stopped and she twisted her head as though she was ducking below the edge of her headpiece to see.

She excused herself from her conversation and made her way through the crush of people to Holly. She clapped her hands together and skipped-walked across the room, the people parting the sea around her. She was an impressive woman, Holly had to give her mother that much.

"Mother," she said and they kissed cheeks.

Her mother held Holly's hands and stood back to get a look at her outfit. "Well, isn't this a surprise. I wasn't sure you were going to make it over here today. Your father tells me you have so much work to do with your little ice cream place."

"It would be easier to finish if you hadn't cut off my finances."

"You know very well that I did it for your own good," she said, even though Holly knew her mother only wanted to bend Holly's will. "You look beautiful in this dress." She pulled her in and whispered into Holly's ear, "Today of all days, you know better than to show up here dressed like it's some sort of nightclub." Backing off, she plastered a fake grin. "What a happy day it is."

This was always how it was with her mother. Holly could do nothing right. It was her father who always had Holly's best interests at heart. "Is Dad here?"

"He's where he always is: at the bar," her mother said and rolled her eyes in that direction. "Catch up with me later. I have a surprise for you."

"Mother, please tell me it's not some man?"

She responded by miming zipping closed her mouth and walked away.

Holly knew days like today were important for the future of the farm and she knew better than to cause any kind of distraction, but whatever her mother had up her sleeve could threaten to push Holly to the brink. For now, she would mind her manners. The farm relied on a constant influx of investor's dollars, and any sucker with enough dough could buy into the idea of owning the next Triple Crown winner. Today's event was a show-and-tell, and she knew exactly the part she was required to play. As much as her mother deserved to be brought down a peg, Holly wouldn't do anything to risk the business.

"Daddy," she greeted her father and reached around his torso for a mimosa. "I see you're getting an early start."

He held his lowball filled with a finger of scotch and swirled the amber liquid around the glass. "Someone's got to do the hard work around here." He chuckled deep down in his chest. "I hate these things," he spoke softly and raised a brow.

"Me too," she said, and they turned into the room. "How are you doing, Dad? Mother says you've been out of town a lot."

"She never likes it when I travel too much. You know how she is about planes or trains. If only she could take a horse everywhere." He raised his glass and greeted an older man with silver hair as he and Holly walked through the crowd, although they spoke like they were the only two in the room. They stopped in front of the floor to ceiling windows that over-looked the expansive green pastures. "I'm being tapped by the Reserve for a special project."

"Dad, that's great," she said and hugged him. "What is it?"

"I can't really talk about it. But it's a great opportunity. It also means that I'll be between here and Manhattan for the rest of the summer and probably into the fall."

"Even better, I can come into town with you and do some shopping."

"Will you have much time to travel once the creamery opens?"

Holly hadn't even considered what her schedule would look like once her shop was open for business. She was so consumed with getting the renovations complete that she failed to think past it. "I suppose I won't. At least not right away."

"You'll find your rhythm soon enough. You know how proud I am that you're following your own path?"

"Thanks, Dad." She knew he meant it, though he couldn't always show it.

"And I'm sorry about the money. I hope you have what you

need for now, and this whole thing with your mother will blow over."

"It'll blow over when I give in to what she wants. I know it hasn't been easy between you two since I came back to town."

"You know she just wants what she thinks is best for you."

"Yeah, so long as my life looks exactly like hers," Holly said and took a long sip of her mimosa. There was nothing wrong with the life her mother had, but raising horses was her mother's passion, not Holly's. Having an appreciation for the creatures would never make up for how much she detested the equestrian business. "Do you think she'll ever come around and accept me for me?"

Her dad chuckled. "Maybe, when she tries your spiced pistachio ice cream?"

Holly clinked her glass against her dad's and leaned her head on his shoulder. They watched the horses being led out from the stables and into the pasture. Their handlers stood just inside the bright white fence that separated the animals from the manicured grounds and directed the horses. Seeing the unbridled horses run and play among the grasses with the same exuberance and freedom as small children, had always captured her imagination.

Holly felt a connection to a horse's determination to express their unique personality despite their confined existence. In her youth, she and Millie experienced a similar joy when they would run alongside the fencing and chase after the horses. Every day was a day of exploration and ease. It was no wonder her mother wished Holly to be a part of the business, as she watched her daughter grow up among the stables and dirt tracks of the farm.

"They really are magnificent, aren't they?" Holly said.

"You've always loved this part, even as a little girl, holding on to my neck as I held you up to see over the fences, your eyes would light up, just as they are now," her dad said and was right.

"Everything's going to work out. You just keep doing what you're doing, and I'll handle your mother."

"She can't say no to this face." Holly pinched her dad's cheek with her free hand. "Can she?" She hugged her dad from the side while he slipped a wad of folded bills between her fingers and the glass. "Dad—"

"To get you through the next few days," he said and winked.

It was uncouth to count the money then and there, but she was sure it looked like several hundred dollars at least. She slid the bills into her dress' pocket and nodded a thanks to her dad.

To her left, one of the staff slid open the panels of glass, collapsing the windows into a pocket inside the wall and causing the space to become an indoor-outdoor room. The sticky breeze took no time to overtake the cool air conditioning. Holly dabbed the back of her hand against her cheeks and forehead to set her makeup and make sure her face wasn't in danger of melting off. It wasn't terribly hot, but it was the most humid day she had felt in a while. Summer was in full swing as the days rolled through to the end of June, that was for sure.

Holly's dad downed his drink and placed it on an unoccupied cocktail table on his way to meet up with her mother. The several dozen guests began to make their way out onto the veranda and down the stairs to the dirt track surrounding the pasture. This was the main event, the review. The next two hours would either make or break the farm's success for the next year. Of course, her parents could make ends meet, but the better the horses showed this year, the better the next year would be, and so on.

Holly waited until many of the guests had found their ideal viewing location before taking her spot. Some people lined up right against the fence railing while others took up elevated positions from bistro tables set up on the veranda. Holly headed to her favorite corner where the white fence and the gate came together. From the vantage point off to one end, she could keep tabs on all the goings on, overhear conversations, and know where her mother was, just in case Holly needed to spill some overheard tea or, conversely, to stay away if need be.

This was her role, a glorified eavesdropping spy. It never ceased to amaze her how freely some people will speak about private matters when they think no one of consequence is listening. For her sake, she blended in amongst the other club members, and since half of the people at the event were new around there, no one would recognize her as a Hollis. Once someone found out who she was related to, the sucking up would start.

Holly stepped up onto the bottom fence rail and rested her arms on the top one. From her position she scanned the faces, some obscured behind hats, for anyone she knew. She was always looking for faces she recognized. She would probably need to dig into the psychology behind that particular tic, but she supposed it was the same as when a person checks out the exits in a theater or when someone takes the stairs instead of the elevator. It was a precaution to know the way out of a situation. And in Holly's case, she never knew when she would need someone to make a run with.

Without Millie romping around with her, she had no one with whom to escape. For now, she intended to enjoy watching the horses show off their beauty and speed. The first horse, a dapple-grey called Marshmallow, with a pedigree tracing back to Giacomo, took to the near pasture. The trainer walked beside the two-year-old colt and directed him to parade by the spectators. Marshmallow was her favorite horse in the stables, and if she had the funds, she might have wanted to own this one herself if for no other reason than to let him run free, but it was to be someone else's turn for now.

"He's a gorgeous one," a low voice came from behind her. For a split second she thought it might be Teddy, but the tone was raspier than Teddy's smooth baritone she was used to hearing.

Coming up behind her before she could turn, two hands

covered hers where she was holding onto the top rail of the fence. He pulled himself up to the same rail, blanketing her body with his from behind. His inky scent was unmistakable. "Hello, Rinaldi." She ducked under one of his arms and scooted down the railing a bit, evading his attempt to hem her in.

"Surprise, baby. Your mother told me you might be here," he whispered into her neck.

"She did, did she?" Holly backed off and spotted her mother speaking to someone down the line. It was obvious that her mother's plan all along had been to get Holly to the farm for such a moment as this. "I have no idea why my being here would have any effect on you whatsoever."

"Oh, don't be like that, baby. You know how sorry I am—"

"For cheating on me while we were on holiday in Split last year?"

"It wasn't what you thought. I swear it, baby. You got to give me a chance to make it up to you." Rinaldi batted his beautiful ebony eyes at her, and she nearly fell back into the abyss.

Nearly. His skin was the color of Mediterranean clay, and his eyes matched his silky hair, kept slicked back from his face. Whoever molded this man did a good job, there was no use in denying how nice he was to look at, but he was rotten to the core. She was only glad that she had seen it before being trapped inside an unhappy relationship.

Rinaldi was the son of a billionaire investor who had used his family's wealth to buy some success in owning horses. The way Rinaldi saw it, the more horses, the better chance he had of winning a Crown. It was quantity over quality with him and horses, and apparently with him and women also.

"I'm not interested in bringing up the past, and frankly, I'm not sure what you hoped to gain by ambushing me here. Are you in the market for a new horse, or a new filly?" she asked and watched the trainer take Marshmallow to the far pasture.

"I was hoping for both," he said in a sultry tone, that she knew too well.

She was a sucker for a man who knew what he wanted. She turned and looked at him. He looked at her right eye, then at her mouth and back up to her left. The intimate way he saw into her was more than she wished to feel for the person who had broken her heart and destroyed her trust in men. But he was so damn irresistible. She had learned her lesson the hard way, but now she knew what she didn't want in a relationship.

"I can forgive you for what you did. I have in fact, even though you don't deserve so much as an ounce of anything from me. Don't think for one second that you can swoop back into my life and convince me you aren't the snake I know you are."

"I might be a snake, baby, but you're no picnic either. I just know we had something good. You know?" he said, and she looked past his face to the next horse, an auburn colt with a black mane.

"How about that one? You and he could be twins," she said, wanting him to remove his gaze from her for a moment long enough for her to take a deep breath.

He didn't bite and stayed locked onto her. "You know we're good together. And our families are practically royalty. We would be the power couple to beat all power couples. Don't you want that?"

He left her with the clearest choice. She could have the life her mother wanted for her, or she could have a life as a small business owner struggling to carve out a piece of the American dream for herself. He offered an enticing proposal to the naïve girl she was a year ago, but she wasn't that girl anymore. "A few weeks ago, I might have entertained the idea, but if I'm honest, I'm not the woman you fell in love with, and I want something more for myself."

"I can give you everything you want. You want to go back to school, done. You want to have that ice cream place you always talked about? I can make that happen and you wouldn't even have to work. You want a ring that would drown you in the ocean? You can have two. I just want you back, baby."

Holly hopped down from the fence railing and her heel sunk down into a soft spot in the dirt. "No," she said and removed the strap from her ankle. With her shoes in her hand, she turned and walked away from Rinaldi.

"No? What do you mean, no?" he said and took chase. "Baby—"

"For starters, I hate that you call me baby." She stomped forward, passing her dad who witnessed the commotion over his shoulder for a second. "I can't stand the way you ogle every set of big tits you see when you think I'm not paying attention, and don't even get me started on you thinking money will fix everything." She stopped and faced him. By now, an audience had taken interest in their quarrel. "You need to find yourself a girl who will appreciate all those things about you, and I'm just not that person. Not today. Not ever."

He reached out for her hand and dropped to one knee.

She snatched her hand away just as fast. "Why don't you go pick yourself a new horse. At least you can leave with one thing you came for today." It felt good to speak her mind. Holly curtsied in mockery at his royalty comment. "Sir," she said and walked away, ignoring the staring eyeballs, and made a line straight to her mother.

"How could you?" Holly said as she passed by her.

"Blake, I … Come back here. I am not chasing you," she whisper-yelled from somewhere in Holly's wake.

Holly marched up the veranda stairs and stopped at the bar inside where she took a mimosa and downed it in one gulp. Her mother met up with her by the time she finished swallowing the fizzy orange drink. She had no intention of hearing whatever sorry explanation her mother was about to offer.

"I don't know who you think you are," her mother said as she met Holly beside the bar. "This is a good merger. You should consider his offer?"

It was even worse than Holly had imagined. "A merger? Do you even hear yourself? You mean a marriage, right? I can't believe you concocted all of this. It wasn't just a surprise; it was an ambush. And you said you weren't sure I was going to be here today ... Dad told you I was coming. Didn't he?"

"Blake. I just want you to be happy—"

"No, Mother, you want me to be you," Holly said. "When are you going to see that no matter how much you want me to be something else, I never will. I love you, but you need to start believing in the person I am and not the person you wish I was." She felt liberty in blowing a hole in the perfect façade her mother had built around herself, but there was a sadness too at the realization that this is all their relationship would likely ever be: one disappointment after another.

"I'm sorry you feel that way," her mother said with a fake grin.

"You're just sorry that I made a scene at your stupid party. It's your fault though. Did you think I would feel pressure from you cutting me off and having all these people around so that I would just say yes to him, and we could all have a celebratory drink or two afterwards. You, as the proud mother-of-the-bride-to-be, and me as the glowing woman who was given the keys to the world?" Holly took two more mimosas and handed one to her mother. "Well, congratulations. You just ruined any chance of me trusting you again."

Holly skipped the toasting and drank the whole thing. She slammed the glass on the counter and the stem broke in half, causing it to crash against the wooden surface. She turned and walked out the front door, not sure when she would return to one of her favorite places on earth, now tainted by her mother's scheming.

This is how Teddy must have felt when she worked to undermine him, she thought. The sun beat down on her with the same heat she felt boiling up in her heart. A mixture of heavy sadness, like the humidity clogging her lungs, and the freedom she felt, like a breeze kissing her skin, reassured her that the easiest road probably is the wrong one.

She was looking forward to her date with Teddy more than ever now and wanted nothing more than for him to hold her in his arms.

CHAPTER 21

THEODOR CHECKED THE TIME ON HIS PEUGEOT ONE MORE TIME. IT was official, it didn't look like Holly was coming. So much for turning the page on their budding romance. If friends can become enemies, and go back to being friends again, then what was to stop Holly and him from becoming enemies for a second time? He felt stupid for trusting her. She really seemed to be into him, but now he was just a loser being stood up by the prom queen.

It was too early for him to go to sleep, though he looked at his bed on the other side of the room like it could solve all his issues to have a whole night's rest. Since deciding to open his chocolaterie, he hadn't slept an entire eight-hour stretch. At first his mind was plagued with all the planning and to-do lists, then he lost sleep over his across-the-street rival, now he would be replaying every interaction he had shared with Holly, wondering where it all went wrong.

He flipped his phone around in his hand. There was no way she was as bad as he thought her to be. During the firefly parade, she had shown a different side of herself to him. She was vulnerable and carefree. No way was that woman who was so gleeful about catching a lightning bug, the same woman who would stand him up now.

Opening his messages, he texted her to see if she was alright. After staring at the screen, the text stayed on 'delivered'. If she read it and then ghosted him, at least he could deal with it. Perhaps something had happened, or she was somewhere where she couldn't write back. She had her event at the farm earlier, but he looked at his timepiece again, it should have ended hours ago. Perhaps Alfonso would know where Holly was, or he could get in touch with Holly's right-hand, Millie.

There was nothing to do but march up to Harbour House and find Alfonso. Taking his linen shirt off the hook by the front door, he opened the door only to find Holly standing on the other side of the threshold. Black mascara painted her cheeks with streaks, and her eyes were red. What he assumed had been a pretty yellow dress at one point, was limp against her body and her hair sat in a messy pile at the crown of her head. Once the shock came and went, he pushed the door completely open.

"Sorry, I think I'm late," she said, and he felt convicted by his shame at having thought she could be capable of standing him up in the first place. "Can I come in?"

He couldn't say a thing. Her appearance begged a dozen questions, but it wasn't until she stepped under the glow of the ceiling light that he saw the extent of her pain. "Holly, your shoulders are really burned. What happened?"

She plopped down on the end of his bed. Her eyes stared blankly ahead into the room.

Without being asked, Theodor went into protector mode. Every nerve in his body was firing, telling him to take care of this helpless creature. He took a clean washcloth and doused it in cold water. Sitting on the edge of the mattress and beside her, he placed the cool rag on her sunburn, being careful not to rub it. "It looks like you walked through the desert today. This is bad."

"I don't feel a thing," Holly said in a monotone and breathy voice.

"You will later. I thought you were at the farm today?" Theodor said and moved the wet cloth to the other shoulder. Her strapless dress had done nothing to shield her from a blazing sun. He unzipped the top inch of the back of her dress and saw the demarcation between her fair skin where it had been protected and the angry, torched skin that hadn't been. "Did someone hurt you?"

"I was so upset. And my car's in a ditch."

He moved the rag again. "Holly, you're not making sense. I need some more information." Her eyes caught his. Tears pooled in her waterline, and he used the back of his finger to wipe them away. Using the damp cloth, he cleaned the mascara from her cheeks and soothed her skin. "That's better."

"I never want to see my mother again." Holly straightened her spine and the skin on her back took an almost purple hue.

"Let me rinse this out," Theodor said and walked back across the room to the small kitchenette where the sink was. "I might have some aloe too. Keep telling your story." He dug around in the bathroom while she continued.

"She surprised me with more than just horses. She and my ex ambushed me with basically a proposal. He said he would give me everything I want, and then he tried to drown me with a ring."

Theodor was rightly confused, but one thing he was certain about, she had come to him with her woes. And that made him feel good about where they were with their relationship. "I feel like there's more," he said and returned to her side with the green aloe gel. "May I?" he asked with his finger resting on her zipper.

She nodded. Theodor unzipped the dress down past her waist, exposing her bare back and the hardly visible tan line from her bikini strings. The previously sun kissed skin looked like nothing compared to the burn area. He swiped the extra pillows from the mattress surface, and she laid down on her belly. Her bare feet dangled off the end of the bed, which he didn't mind because they were so dirty.

"You said no, to the proposal?" Theodor squirted the gel into his hand and warmed it just a little with the heat of his palms. He began at the center of her back and used minimum pressure to smooth the aloe over her skin, careful not to create any friction.

She relaxed under his touch and sucked some air through her teeth.

"Sorry, it's cold," he said.

"No, it feels good. Keep going and I'll keep talking."

"Sounds good to me," he said and realized he shouldn't enjoy touching her skin as much as he was under these conditions, but it felt good to care for her. A few minutes earlier, he had been livid and hurt that she had stood him up, now he was prepared to scorch earth for her.

"So, I get to the farm, and boy, do I wish you had come with me. Or Millie, or heck, even Alfonso. At least I wouldn't have been alone when Rinaldi propositioned me to get back together. I don't know why he ever thought he could just show up and expect me to fall back into his arms like some simpering little girl."

"Rinaldi is your ex? Did you deck him?"

"How could I? We were in front of all these potential investors and buyers. Honestly, I was so insulted that he and my mother thought that's all it would take for me to change the trajectory of my life. I was beside myself. I told my mother we were done, and I got in my car and headed here."

"Holly, that was hours ago." Theodor wasn't sure how far away the farm was from the Cove, but he knew it was nearby.

"Once I got in the car, I got myself all worked up and started crying."

He hated that she was so upset, even now, he could hear the strain in her throat.

"I don't know what's worse, feeling set-up like that, or feeling so alone."

"You're not alone," he whispered. "I'm here."

She flipped her head over, her blonde hair falling over her face. He moved a strand away from her wet eyes. "I didn't want you to think I forgot about our date. So, after I ran my car into a ditch, I walked the rest of the way."

"Why didn't you call me? Or anyone else. I would have come to get you."

"I couldn't find my phone. I don't know whether I left it at the farm, or it got tossed in the car when I ran off the road. Plus, I thought I was a lot closer to town than I was. It's not like I'd take a ride from a stranger."

"Someone offered you a ride?"

"Yeah, some old guy in a blue truck. He seemed a little too happy to pick me up, so I told him no thank you and that I was fine. Maybe if I'd been wearing shoes, I would have been more convincing, but I told him I wanted to walk, and he moved on."

"I wonder if that was Pa, the old guy that works here. He drives a blue pickup, but he would have sent help."

"He asked if there was anyone he could call, and I told him I was fine. I kind of was at the time, but I thought I was a lot closer to here than I was."

Theodor traced his eyes down Holly's backside and legs to her bare feet. Dust coated her ankles to her toes. He used the washcloth, still damp, and cleaned them off. "You're a mess."

She cried at his accusation. "I know I am. I only pretend to have it all together. I skip through life just hoping that everything will work out every day. And most of the time it does." She flipped over and perched up on her elbows to keep the aloe off the white duvet. "You're the only person that really challenges me. You don't buy into my fake side."

"Would you really want me to?"

"I used to think that's all I was to someone; the trophy meant to look and act the part. But it's exhausting playing a role. That's all Rinaldi wanted me for. He actually tried to convince me to be with him by tempting me with the exact opposite of what I want. He offered me a big ring, big enough to drown me. He wanted to pay for my creamery to open, basically with me as a pretty figurehead. And after all that, he said we would be royalty."

"Sounds like a pretty sweet deal to me. Where can I sign up for the Rinaldi special?" His laugh was infectious, and her sad tears turned to happy ones.

She sat up and held the front of her dress across her chest with one hand while playfully hitting his shoulder with the other. He caught her hand against his beating heart so that she could feel it. Their breathing synced up and a quiet gravity descended on the room.

"Can I have a loose shirt to wear?" she asked, and her cheeks flushed.

"I have a better idea."

Theodor knew just what this woman needed, and it had nothing to do with putting more clothing on. Knowing she needed to have something covering her body for his idea to work, he grabbed an oversized T-shirt from his dresser beside the bed and threw it at her. "You can put this on for now."

Holly didn't move from her spot in the middle of his bed. She sat up on her knees and slid the shirt over her head. The thin white fabric fell over her shoulders and chest down below her hips. She stood with her dirty feet on the white covers, and he didn't even care. He swallowed hard as she shimmied her dress down her legs and kicked it from her pointed toes in his direction. Catching the yellow floral frock in his hand, he could smell the remnants of her vanilla perfume still in the fibers.

He tossed the garment to the floor where he preferred it to stay and offered his hand to her. She jumped down and he caught her at her waist, not wanting to cause any more pain or injury to her burned shoulders and chest. She took his hand and threaded her fingers in his.

At the door, Theodor nudged her a pair of flip-flops with his foot, even though they were far too large, it was cute seeing her wear his items. He slid on a pair of boat shoes, the same ones he had planned on wearing to their previously planned date that night. He was glad she was there, even if she was late, and even if she was miserable. She had come to him when she could have gone to anyone.

She was his. For now, at least, and Theodor intended to make the most of whatever time they had together.

He led Holly outside and down the path towards the shore. The stars had come out and twinkled like heavenly spotlights on their evening. The afternoon heat had given way to a comfortable breeze that he hoped was helping her angry skin feel better.

"Where are we going?" she whispered, and an excited little giggle escaped her throat like they were doing something they shouldn't.

The outdoor areas at the Foundry were deserted, compared to the previous night when the firefly parade had the whole property abuzz with action. No, tonight, they had the cove to themselves. He brought her down the shore past the dock to a section that was surrounded on three sides by clumps of dense bushes. The area was dark, and but for her blind trust in him, she should have been apprehensive but didn't appear to be.

She held onto his arm and huddled near him as they shuffled down the short embankment. "Teddy, what are we doing down here?"

The cove water was like glass, reflecting with an artist's accuracy every single star from above. The crescent moon shone like a beacon near the horizon and created a long shadow behind Holly. Theodor stepped into the water first and a hundred ripples burst out from the disturbance. Without speaking a word, he slid his shirt over his head and tossed it over to a nearby fallen tree.

Holly giggled again, and he desperately wanted to find the spot on her neck where the delicious sound originated.

He unbuttoned his shorts and slid them down his legs. They ended up beside the shirt on the log and he walked backwards into the water wearing only his blue boxer-briefs. "Your turn." He teased, knowing full well that she wore nothing but light-pink lace panties beneath his shirt.

"Turn around," she said and all he could hear was the sound of cotton rustling against her skin and hair and landing on the tree with his. Her toes splashed in the water's edge and a large ripple came around his upper body. She was in the water, and she was nearby. "Alright. You can look now."

He wanted to see her; he was a man, after all, who wished she wasn't wholly submerged. But he took a deep breath and let the moment rest. From the way the current hit him below the surface, he came around to where he knew she would be waiting for him. To his displeasure, Holly was well hidden to her shoulders by the water's shell, but a smile graced her pretty face.

Her eyes were closed, and she bobbed up and down. "This feels really good on my burn."

"I'm sorry I wasn't there for you today. If I had been, maybe none of this would have happened."

Her eyes flew open. "Rinaldi still would have happened. And I had already been out in the sun for too long before the whole car thing—"

"Ended up in a ditch and forced you to walk here for hours?"

"Yeah. That." She laughed. "Don't feel bad that you weren't with me at the farm. You're here for me now, that's what matters."

Theodor was careful to keep his distance from her naked body. Even though it was dark and private. He didn't want to push his luck when they were finally on the right track. "Can I be honest? I thought you stood me up earlier."

"And that made you feel mad?"

"Sad. Hurt. I guess I just like you more than I wanted to admit." Because he thought he might love this woman. "And now, knowing what you went through this afternoon, I feel terrible about that."

"You really like me?" she asked and came closer to him. He backed off but she pursued him further. "You're not just saying what I want to hear and making me fall in love with you?"

"Are you?" he asked as her hands swiped up his arms. His heart was beating so fast he could see new ripples forming on the water around him. "In love with me?"

"What if I am?"

"Then I'd say we probably shouldn't be skinny-dipping in the dark." Because his body craved her touch, and she deserved a man who wouldn't use her body to manipulate her emotions.

"I don't know if I can say that I'm falling in love with you, Theodor Black, but I can tell you that I love the way you make me laugh." She kissed his cheek, and his eyes closed to savor the sensation. "I love how we share a passion for sugary things." She licked his lip as if she would find something sweet there. He was frozen. "I love how you think I'm a better person than I am."

He captured her face in his hands. "You're the most frustrating person I've ever met, Blake Holly Hollis." They paused, reading each other's next move. The night seemed to stand still but for the chirping crickets filling the air with music. He could take her right there. He could have her in his arms and make her forget about Rinaldi or any other guy she'd ever known. He could fill the night air with her moans and sounds of his name. But ... he backed off. "I think—"

"We should slow down a bit?" she finished.

"Yes," he said and stood up and walked out of the water. He tugged his shirt onto his wet skin and slid his shorts back on.

Holding his other shirt up to her, he said, "Come on out of there."
He turned his head and squeezed his eyes shut.

Holly took the shirt, and he hoped she would put it on in the
interim time. "Can I sleep over?" she asked, and he cracked an eye
at her. "No funny business," she added.

"I'll take the floor."

CHAPTER 22

With a sunburn as bad as Holly's, she had little hope of finding a comfortable sleeping position. She had at best, entered that state between sleep and awake, when the mind wanders through a slow world. She was acutely aware of the man sleeping feet away from her on the floor. Teddy's breathing acted as a calm reminder that she was in a safe place, while the throb of her skin kept her mind planted on the wrong side of slumber.

Waking meant she would have to go. Back to Millie's. Back to work. Back to the place where she struggled with trusting anyone. She cracked an eyelid, not enough to see the room, but enough to let the first blue shades of dawn in. It was morning, and it was the first day of her new life, resigned to the fact that she was a capable woman who could make her own way in life.

The best part of her new beginning was that she wasn't truly alone. She had gone to the farm under the false assumption that her mother wanted what was best for her and left feeling alone in her ambition. Now, from her position laying on her belly, she peeked over the side of the bed at the man she was falling for, and knew she wasn't solo anymore. She had Teddy. She had Millie, Alfonso, and even her dad would cheer her on.

Most of all, she just wished she had treated Teddy better from the start. Weeks had gone by, wasted, when they could have been building each other up, and all she did was work against him. It had been fun at first. She sneaked around, painted his sign, stole his workers, and taken her pranks too far when she attempted rerouting his product delivery. Regret was evident in her bones that ached just looking at the sweet man and his pinched brows.

He cracked an eye open, and she was caught. "Morning," he said in a low raspy voice. He stretched his arms out wide, and his covers fell to the side. His exposed chest, tan from the day when they had their water balloon fight, looked like soft silk, and his dark chest hairs shadowed his toned muscles. His hair was loose around his face, and he smiled up at her. "Did you sleep at all?"

"Not much. Everything feels like sandpaper against my skin," she said and sat up while holding the crisp ivory sheet over her bare chest. She hadn't worn anything other than her panties in an attempt to reduce any friction on her burn. "Can you put more aloe on my back before I go?"

He sat up on his haunches beside the bed and nodded. A devilish one-sided smirk revealed a sliver of his white teeth, and he used his pointer finger to call her down to his level.

She knew what he wanted, because she wanted it more. She leaned down to him, so slowly he probably thought she was teasing, but because she was taking care with her tender skin. A few inches to go, he nudged her closer with the same finger under her chin and crushed his lips against hers. Morning breath aside, his pillowy mouth was the softest thing she had touched in hours. Heat spread through her as he caressed her with his mouth. He was tender and slow, not taking more than she gave. Maybe she *was* in love with this man.

The kiss, as satisfying as it was, ended with alarm bells.

Holly was the first to pull away. They looked around the room for the source of the screeching sounds. The noise wasn't coming from anywhere inside. She wrapped the sheet around her body and wobbled to the window. The sirens emanated from over the hill in the direction of town.

"Main Street," they said in unison.

Forgoing the aloe gel, she grappled for yesterday's dress and slid the light-weight yellow layers up her body, removing the sheet as she went. Teddy zipped up the back without her needing to ask and she sucked air in through her teeth when the top seem of the strapless dress pressed into her burnt skin. Taking the side seams at her hips in her hands, she tugged the dress down just enough to get the material off of her sore flesh.

"Shoes?" Teddy asked and presented a pair of flip flops.

"Thanks," she said and slid her feet into the brown leather sandals. "What do you think it is?"

"Sounds like a fire truck, maybe?" Teddy walked to the window and moved the white curtains out of his view. "There's smoke!" he shouted. "Shit. My roasters. Maybe I didn't turn them off yesterday." He threw on his sweatshirt and slid his boat shoes onto his feet as he scrambled for his phone. "Shit, shit, shit."

Holly stopped his frantic body, and she took his face in her hands. "It could be anything, and we won't know until we get over there." She took his hand. "Let's go."

They hurried up the road, half walking and half jogging, but holding hands the entire time. They turned the corner on to Main and stopped short. Two huge firetrucks were parked directly in their path and spraying water, not into Teddy's shop, but into the second story of Holly's building.

She began to run but he held her back. "What are you going to do? Run into a fire?"

She collapsed into his arms. "This can't be happening. Not when I was so close to opening" Her tears fell freely and soaked through his thin shirt. He rubbed his hand through her hair as she wept. Thank god she was with Teddy right now or she didn't know what she would do. "I have to see the damage."

"Of course, you do. And Holly, look at me. Whatever happens, we will work to fix it. You're not alone," he said and kissed her forehead.

He had no idea how much she needed to hear those words from him. She had underestimated him in so many ways, least of all how big his heart really was. If she felt like she was falling in love with him before, she felt like she was ready to shout it from the charred rooftop of her shop.

Teddy led the way down the sidewalk on the opposite side of the road from her shop. As they approached, the full extent of the damage materialized. Blackened water dripped from the eaves and her sign above the front door was stained from the flames that had licked the painted surface. Her front windows lay in shattered shards across the sidewalk and allowed her to see inside.

Through the mist of spraying water, men in yellow coats moved through the space. She stood, wrapped in Teddy's arms with nothing else to do but watch her dreams turn to ash before her. "I can't take it, Teddy. You watch for me." He let her bury her face in his chest and cry. "I deserve this. It's karma."

"What do you know about karma?" he said, and she felt a chuckle vibrate from deep within his chest.

"Don't laugh at me. This isn't a time for jokes," she said through her tears. "I treated you so badly. I even told you that I hoped your shop would burn down. What else could this be but the universe mocking me. I'm a good person, I swear it."

"I don't think the universe is out to get you, Holly."

"I do," she cried and wondered how many more tears she had. Her face was wet, and so was Teddy's grey T-shirt. "I'm supposed to open in a few days. There's no way I can do that now. And if I don't open on time, I can't win the grant money."

"You're still concerned with the grant? At a time like this? Oh, honey." He pushed her away enough to look into her eyes. "All that matters is that you weren't here when the fire started."

"Excuse me, folks. I need you to back up," a firefighter said.

"Wait," Holly said and turned to the older man. "That's my place. Please."

"Ma'am. I'm so sorry. Are you alright?" he asked and pointed to his own chest and then to hers.

She looked down at her reddened skin. "I'm alright. This is an unrelated sunburn. Can you tell me what happened? I know all my equipment was off yesterday. The electricians had some work to do. Was it the electricians? I need to know who to sue."

"Ma'am. I can't say for certain until the investigation is complete, there's always a chance that fires like this one may have been arson."

"Arson?" Holly shouted. "You mean someone did this to me on purpose?"

"We don't know for sure, but it is standard procedure to examine all causes."

"When can I go in?" she said.

"Later today. Where can we reach you?"

"Right here. I'm not leaving this spot until I know more."

The firefighter understood and walked back to the scene.

"Arson? Is he serious?" she said knowing Teddy knew nothing more than she did yet. "Who would have a motivation to burn down a creamery? It doesn't make sense to me. Do you think it was one of the other shop owners? Do you think it was …" she paused and looked at Teddy's eyes, searching for a trace of guilt.

"Woah! Woah! Holly. Why are you looking at me like that? Whatever you're thinking you'd better stop going down that road right now." His words were a warning, but it may have been too late. "You can't possibly think that I …"

She backed away from him. The damage was done. She had considered him guilty for only a fraction of a second. "Only because I can't be totally sure I wouldn't have burned your place down if I believed it would have helped me in some way. If I'm capable of doing something so heinous, then why couldn't you have?"

"Holly. You're digging yourself into a hole that I'm not sure you can get out of here." Another warning.

"I'm sorry," she knew admitting that she had experienced that singular thought was enough to destroy the trust they had built. "I know you didn't do this. You were with me the whole time."

"Then why did you even think it? Why do you expect the worst in everyone around you?"

That was the fifty-thousand-dollar question, and she had no capacity to come up with an answer when her eyes were glued to the sopping exterior of the Cups & Cones Creamery.

"Let me know when you have a better answer for me. In the meantime, I have work to do."

CHAPTER 23

Holly wasn't sure how long she had sat on the curb watching the firefighters work, but no stretch of time could help her go back and take back the thought that Teddy had anything to do with the fire. All the while she sat there, she had been too cowardly to look over her shoulder and see him. She knew he was there, just like he had said he would be. She wasn't alone, but he hadn't said anything to her all morning. He was likely waiting for her to give a better explanation for having accused him of arson.

Workers came and went into the chocolaterie behind her, one even brought her a bottle of water, no doubt at Teddy's direction. He wasn't speaking to her, but he was still caring for her. His actions spoke louder than words ever could, but her words alone had cut. It seemed she could do nothing to get out of her own way.

As she waited for the all-clear to inspect the damage, the sounds coming from Teddy's kitchen kept her company; metal pans clinking on a stainless counter, cardboard boxes ripping open and bubble wrap popping. The rich scent of his chocolates seeped out through his open door and out to the sidewalk where she remained. The mouth-watering aroma was hardly enough to overtake the bitter smell of charred wood coming from her shop on the other side of the street.

The fire chief came out of her front door with a sort of pipe in his hands, and locked eyes with her. She stood and crossed the road blocked off by a fire truck parked perpendicular to the sidewalks His lifted brows and relaxed jaw gave her hope that she could get inside.

"We're all done in there, but before you go in, there's some good and bad news." He handed her the narrow, pipe-like object. "The good news, it wasn't arson. This thing here is what caused the fire, old knob-and-tube wiring in the upper section of the wall."

"And the bad news?"

"You probably would have never known otherwise, but there was an extensive network of carpenter ants that had turned the wood to pulp in the same area. In my opinion, the shavings dried out and came into contact with this old wiring. It was a matter of time at that point. It's just a good thing no one was here at the time."

"So, it really was an accident?"

He nodded. "I'm glad to say so. Before you go in, you'll need to take a few precautions. My inspection team says the structure is stable except for the Eastern corner of the upper floor, but I would recommend having this designated a hard hat area until an engineer gives the all-clear. As for the downstairs area, the damage is minimal, just wet. And here," he pulled out a white and yellow face mask from a pocket on his coat sleeve, "Wear this today. The wind will clear out the smoke in a few hours."

"Thanks, chief." Holly watched the crews load up in their trucks and toot their horn as they left. She was left in the middle of the street to take in the extent of her loss.

Dozens of people had gathered outside the cordoned-off area and were whispering and pointing at her shop. In addition to the smoky show, a bullseye might as well have been painted in red all over her skin. There was no hiding from this. She shrugged her shoulders and waved at the people as she headed in to her shop.

Out of the corner of her eye, she saw Millie pushing through the dispersing crowd and running in Holly's direction. Looking down the street, Holly saw Alfonso close behind. Millie threw her arms around Holly and hugged her in tight. Too tight. "Ouch. Watch my back."

Millie stepped back. "Oh my god. What happened?"

Holly shook her head. "Would you believe me if I told you that it's a long story?"

Millie smiled. "I would. Your stories are usually long. Are you okay? We came through as soon as they let us."

Alfonso finally caught up to them and bent over with his palms bracing on his knees. "Alfonso no run fast."

Millie giggled at Alfonso, and it was nice that she broke the mood, even for a moment. "What can we do to help?"

For the first time since Teddy left her be, she turned and looked to his front door. "Alfonso, can you go across the street and see if Teddy has three hard-hats that we can borrow. I know I have some in the back, but I don't want to risk going in without one."

"Three hats. Come right up!" Alfonso darted across the street and was back in a flash. "Theodor says to return hats whenever. Okay? We go in?"

Holly slipped the white hat over her head and adjusted the strap at the back. "Yes. We go." She might have been ready to go inside, but the real unknown was what she was walking into.

Millie, sensing her apprehension threaded her arm through the crook of Holly's elbow. "We're here."

The small words of assurance were no surprise coming from Millie, but she really wanted Teddy to be beside her too. With one final look over her shoulder at the chocolaterie, Teddy stood shadowed just inside his shop's front door. Catching her gaze, he turned away from her, his action stung exactly how he likely intended. And she deserved it for what she had done.

If her shop burned because of karma, then losing the man she was falling in love with was a cruel joke she had played on herself. One thing she knew about karma was that the laws work both ways. Meaning, if she got *bad* because that's what she put out into the universe, then she had a chance to turn it all around by putting *good* back into the world.

How exactly? She didn't have the brain capacity to think about it, but she knew it would start right here, in the dripping remains of her shop. No matter what the damage, there was no way she was conceding defeat and moving back home. She took the first step across the threshold and another. Her eyes adjusted to the low light, and she was able to see how bad the damage was. Her mural, on the long wall, was intact and she let out a sigh of relief.

Millie and Alfonso worked around the space, righting tables and chairs while Holly headed to the office where she and Millie had piled all the supplies and merchandise a few days prior. She opened the door and saw that the entire stock was intact. Other than a wet space, the damage on this level didn't look too bad.

The fire chief said the blaze sparked on the second floor, where there was nothing but the guts of what she hoped to turn into apartments or even an event space at some future date.

"Hey Millie, I'm going to look upstairs. Can you get started mopping up all the water? I don't want to have to replace brand new floors."

"Already on it," Millie said as she took two mops from the kitchen and passed by Holly.

Holly mouthed her thanks to her most loyal friend.

Before she went up the dark stairs, she propped open the back door. Light flooded in and illuminated the bottom few steps. Once at the landing at the top, she could see what the chief had seen. In the far corner at the front of the building splintered lathe, like monster's teeth, surrounded an exposed cavity. Thin ribbons of light poked through the exterior brick and shined along the moist and blackened vertical wall studs. Holly ran her fingers along the missing mortar. Crouched down, she swished the water around where it pooled on the old laminate flooring.

By the looks of the destruction, it was time to call in some help. The extent of work needed to be completed now was more than she alone could finish before opening day. There was still a couple days until the Chamber of Commerce was scheduled to make their assessment. *What better way to win the grant money than to come back from such an utter disaster*, she thought. Holly felt like, if she could somehow pull this off, the money would be hers.

There was nothing else she could do upstairs, other than to dry it all out. For now, the main dining area was her priority to get cleaned up. The kitchen too. She headed back down to see what Millie and Alfonso had done.

Millie was using a large push broom and sweeping the water out the front door and onto the sidewalk where streaks of gray and brown painted the concrete outside. "How was it up there?"

"Seared like a steak, but without the happy ending." Holly took a mop in her hands and joined Millie in clearing the remaining water off the floor. The broom had done a great job of getting the puddles out. The mop would get the rest. "Where'd Alfonso go?"

"He had to get back to the Foundry. He came on his break to help I wish I could see him for longer stretches, but I guess that's the job."

Holly wondered if Alfonso's in-and-out lifestyle was something she should expect for herself once the shop opened. She couldn't think about that now because opening at all was now up in the air. "You should talk to him about it. See if there's some way to get more time together, but it was nice of him to come help for a few. He's a really good guy."

Millie blushed and she bit her lips between her teeth.

"You really like him?" Holly said and wrung the water from her mop out in the street.

"It's just easy with him." She smiled and shook her head. "Stop it. Okay."

"Fine. It's just nice to see you happy."

"I don't want to jinx anything, but I think things are going well," Millie said, and raised a brow at Holly.

"What?"

"I don't know, maybe the fact that you've been trying your hardest to ruin any chance you have at being happy with a certain chocolatier. And what happened to your skin? You look like you fell in vat of tomato juice."

"I went to the farm yesterday," Holly said with a grimace.

"That bad, huh?"

"I thought I could smooth things over with my mother."

"I'm guessing you didn't?" Millie said.

"Rinaldi was there," Holly said and knew that her friend would put two and two together.

"No! Your mother invited him," Millie said.

Holly squeezed out another load of water and started back inside at the display case. "Yep. And he thought he could convince me to go off and be the it, power couple and rule the horse world together. You know that's not what I want, even if I didn't hate him with a passion, I wouldn't give up all this." She motioned her arms in a wide circle. Laughing, because the tears had long run out.

"How could your mother do that to you? I don't care how much she wants you to be just like her, she would never have given up her dreams for a man. It just worked out that the man she loved, your dad, supported her ambitions."

"It helped that he was already rich," Holly said. "They never had to want for anything. I know they love each other, that's not the issue. I just wish they both loved me for me."

"Your dad does."

171

"Yeah, but I know he's tired of playing defense on my behalf. And I have one more favor I need to call in."

"You can save your favor for another occasion. I hope you don't mind, but I took the liberty of calling a contractor friend of mine, he's also an engineer, which I figured you would need." Millie said. "He said he was on his way now."

"I don't mind at all." Holly hugged her friend. Millie was always putting good out into the world, and Holly intended to learn from her example. "You're such a good friend. I don't know how I got on for so long without you."

"There is something I've been meaning to tell you."

"Lay it on me. It's not like this day can get much worse," Holly said and rang out the mop in the street.

"You remember the day you and Teddy got arrested?"

"What did you do?" Holly said knowing the tone of Millie's voice meant she was feeling guilty about something.

"I was the one who tipped off the cops. I called a friend who works on the force. The arrest was just an effort to get the two of you to figure things out. Please don't hate me."

Holly was too preoccupied with the issue wetting her toes to be mad. The truth was, being arrested seemed like so long ago. "I don't. But how did the charges get dropped? Was that your friend's doing too?"

"Teddy cut a deal," Millie said and propped the broom against the counter. "That's what Alfonso told me anyway."

"Of course he would have done something like that. No wonder the officer called him Saint Theo. I wonder how he did it."

Millie shrugged. "So, you're not mad at me?"

"You were just trying to help me get out of my own way, and I love you for that." Holly hugged her sweaty, burned arms around her friend as sunlight glinted off a windshield in the road. "Is that your guy?" she asked and pointed at a man getting out of a black F-150 parked outside.

Millie's contractor removed his sunglasses as he came through the front door. He extended his hand. "You must be Holly."

She shook his hand and explained the situation and what she needed him to look at. He got right to work inspecting the structure and fire damage. Luckily, there was plenty of other work for Holly to get done while she waited for his report.

"He's really good. I used him when I worked on America and Leo's place. Whatever you need, he'll help you out."

"Let's just hope it's not so much that it'll delay my opening."

Millie took a trashcan out to the sidewalk and handed a pair of rubber gloves to Holly. The sun was hot, not like the day before at the farm, but she wished she had taken Teddy's shirt after all instead of working in a sundress. Together, they picked up the shattered glass panes. No matter what the contractor said, she knew they would need to board these windows up for the night until new glass could be installed.

"Your sunburn looks terrible. You never connected the dots for me." Millie said, and Holly knew she wouldn't let it go.

"After what my mother and Rinaldi did, I left. I ended up putting my car into a ditch and decided to walk back to town. I thought it was way closer than it was."

"I'm so sorry. And you just happened to wear yesterday's dress today?" Millie teased.

"You noticed?"

"You always wear yellow to the farm. Though I don't think you do it intentionally. And I know you wore strapless just to irritate your mother. As for the burn, I'm guessing there's more to tell."

Holly tossed a pie-sized piece of glass into the can. "I was supposed to go out with Teddy last night, so I just walked all the way to his cabin. I didn't want to go anywhere else. And I didn't want him to think I stood him up. It was way late as it was. But when I got to his place, he took care of me and we ..."

"Blake Hollis, what did you do?"

"Nothing."

"Is nothing the reason he isn't here with you right now?"

"No." Holly swallowed her disgrace. "He's not here right now because I accused him of arson this morning."

"You didn't!" Millie gasped.

All Holly could do was nod.

"You were right, this day can't really get much worse for you. What are you going to do about it?" Millie stood as she put all the pieces together. "Oh my god. You love him, don't you."

Holly shrugged and looked across the street, hoping to glimpse his smile or ridiculous man-bun. "It doesn't matter now. I doubt he'll ever forgive me."

Millie snapped her fingers in front of Holly's blank stare. "Earth to Holly. He loves you too. It makes what you did hurt more. All you have to do is apologize. And mean it."

"I have so much to do," Holly said as the contractor approached them out front. His eyes were like slits from his fake smile pushing his cheeks up. "That bad?"

"You want the good news first? It looks like the structure is intact. Some shoring up on the site where the fire started wouldn't be a bad idea but it's sound. Some masonry work and new electrical upstairs should take care of that."

"And the bad?" Holly braced herself on Millie's arm.

"You've got asbestos tiles on the second floor. It's a big job."

"Can I just leave it for now? So long as we don't disturb them?" She put her had together at her chest like she was praying to the reno-gods.

"I'm afraid the fire and water constitute a disturbance. You'll need to get it taken care of before anyone can occupy this space."

"I understand." She removed her yellow rubber glove and shook his hand. "Can we get started now?"

He nodded and pulled out his phone. "I'll line up my guys right now," he said and took his phone from his shirt pocket.

"I don't have much money," Holly dug in her pocket for the wad of cash her dad had slipped to her in the clubhouse. She counted out the Benjamins.

Millie snatched the bills. "Where did you get all this cash, Holly?"

"My dad, and it's all I have left. Will it be enough?"

Millie smiled. "I think it's plenty."

"Don't worry about the details," the man said. "We'll get this place straightened out in no time." He took the money from Millie and walked to his truck.

"I need new glass too!" Holly yelled as though he had missed the giant gaping holes in the front of her store. She turned to Millie and with sheer willpower sucked her tears back into her head. "Let's hope he can get this work done like yesterday."

Millie wrapped her arms around Holly. "We need a drink. Come on, let's take a break."

Holly was in no mood to put up a fight, and the two women walked down the road to the restaurant at the end of the street with one goal in mind—drowning Holly's terrible day in a giant margarita.

CHAPTER 24

FOLLOWING THE BURNING—BOTH HOLLY'S SKIN AND HER BUSINESS —Theodor spent the next three days watching her through his front windows. Sure, he was checking up on her from a distance, but it was hard not to notice the crews coming and going from her store in dance-like precision. As a spectator, there were more than enough happenings across the street to keep him entertained. As a business owner trying to get everything perfect for the soft-opening when the Chamber members would conduct their review, the commotion across the road was an unnecessary distraction.

Tomorrow was the day when Theodor's concept would be tested for the first time. All the weeks of work while dodging Holly's efforts to sabotage him came down to how the next twenty-four hours went. His selections had already been well received at the tasting, the open house, and the chocolate festival at the Foundry, but those events were special occasions. It remained to be seen how the general public would accept a local chocolaterie.

Ignoring yet another pickup truck blocking the sidewalk out front, he stood just inside his front doors and looked at the tall shelf that anchored the rear portion of the shop. He took in the space from the customer's point of view. He had displayed his merchandise over and over again, not satisfied with the impact he hoped the items would have. The vibe he wanted was more dark-academia and less tourist-trap-at-the-boardwalk, but the T-shirts hanging on the adjacent wall were screaming gift-shop.

With a step stool, he reached up and unhooked the hangers from the pegs he had already installed, leaving them empty.

"Maybe you should roll them," Holly's sweet voice said from behind his back and caused his heart to jump.

He hadn't so much as waved at Holly since she accused him of being capable of starting a fire. The only fire he wished to stoke was the one in her soul, but he didn't know if he could forgive her until she apologized. He had a split second to decide how to handle her. He could say something snarky and send her away—which he didn't really want to do—or he could say nothing and see what she wanted. He turned around and had to bite his lip at how good she looked.

It wasn't fair for a person to be as pleasing to gaze upon. Her hair was pinned up in a swirled bun on top of her head with little pieces falling out and framing her rosy cheekbones. He wasn't sure if her blush came from seeing him or if the color was the remnants of the sunburn, though he hoped for her sake that the burn had subsided by now and she was happy to see him.

"May I?" she asked and walked to him. Taking one of the shirts to a small dining table, Holly laid it out and folded the arms in. She flipped it over, performed some kind of magic spell, and presented a rolled shirt with his logo perfectly positioned and visible at the center. She handed it back to him and took the other shirts, repeating her magic. When she was finished, he possessed a stack of rolls that fit nicely inside the confines of one shelf.

"How do you know how to do that?" he asked.

"I worked in the college bookstore," she said and handed him the last item. "Teddy …"

His hand brushed hers in the transfer and his eyes wasted no time to lock onto her glossy lips. "Why are you here?"

"For the obvious reason. I owe you an explanation," she said and backed away. "An apology."

Theodor froze while he waited for her to continue. He watched as she tucked a tendril behind her ear, and he wished he were those fingers so he could touch her face. She straightened the straps of her overalls. Underneath, she wore a tiny floral crop top that exposed the silky flesh around her waist, which he was not ashamed of having committed to his memory.

"Teddy, I'm really sorry for thinking you could have done something so … ugh. I hate that I haven't seen you in days. Do you know how many times I wished for you to just lurk in the shadows if it meant I could see you." She turned and walked towards the door. She chuckled at herself. "This is so embarrassing."

Theodor's body ached to be near her and told him he was willing to forgive her, but it wasn't just that she had doubted him, and she knew it. "You wounded me."

"I know I did. And I know it's so much more than one misplaced thought. I've spent more time than I'm proud of trying to win the grant money at any cost, including destroying you in the process. I guess the joke is on me." She chuckled again but it was pinched in her throat as though she was on the verge of crying. If there was one thing Theodor wasn't strong enough to deal with was her tears. "I got what was coming to me."

"From here, it looks like this little setback hasn't pained you too much. You've had about a dozen trades coming and going—"

"You have no idea what I've been dealing with." She turned and he could see the moisture welling up in her eyes. "The fire wasn't that bad. I could have handled it, but the water did almost as much damage. I had to order all new windows at a rush, there was asbestos everywhere upstairs, and all the electrical had to be upgraded. And if by some miracle I get everything done in time, I have no way to pay for anything else. I'll be lucky if I even have enough ice cream to make it a week."

He swallowed hard. Here he was thinking it was a simple case of replacing a few timbers and drywall while it had been a near complete overhaul. "I didn't know."

"How could you have? You never even came to check in on me. I know you would have given the same courtesy to any other shop owner on this street, but not me." She plopped down at the rustic table at the front window.

Filtered sunlight illuminated her blonde hair like a golden halo. He fought the urge to argue with her, mostly because she was on target. He would have done as she said for others, but he hadn't checked on her, not even once. "You know why I couldn't."

"I get it. You told me you were waiting for me to have a better answer about why I thought you might have something to do with the fire. And I'm sorry I didn't reach out to you sooner."

"I just don't know if I can trust you, Holly. You haven't exactly been—"

"Truthful? Nice? I know," she said and paced in front of the windows. "Believe it or not, you've torn down more of my defenses than I thought was possible. It's almost as though the harder I tried to close off from you, the harder I was falling ..." She wiped a tear off her upper cheek, and he hesitated to hold her. "And I was falling for you, Theodor Black."

He opened his mouth to speak but nothing came out.

She searched his face for a hint of what he was thinking about, but she didn't know that he was picturing scooping her up and throwing her over his shoulder like a neanderthal, taking her back to his cave, and demonstrating to her just how much he loved her. But his doubt froze his feet in place and stitched his mouth shut.

She stood, crossing her arms under her chest. When he stayed mute, she dropped her arms to her side. "I came to apologize, and I have, but I'd like a chance to build some of our trust back. Tonight, eight thirty at the dock?"

He didn't respond, not because he didn't want to, but because he was running every future scenario through his mind. There were a thousand ways he could see them going from rival shop owners to lovers, but so many things could go wrong.

With no answer, she shrugged with a smile and walked out his front door.

He wanted to pull his hair out.

Time was short to get everything prepared for the opening, and now all he could think about was seeing her later. Looking at his shelf, pleased with what she had accomplished, he knew the shop was nearly ready. He still had to fill all the display cases with chocolates and finish setting up the rear patio. It had been a last-minute decision to makeover the modest space, but he thought it would be a great addition to impress the Chamber of Commerce with. It had cost him nothing but sweat. A side benefit was that he could rent out the patio for private tastings, and maybe a couples' chocolate class similar to the one he had set up on the tasting day outside.

If and when he completed the last items on his to-do list, he would then decide whether to meet her at the dock later.

He looked across the street at a gorgeous Roadster that had just pulled up. An older man with salt and pepper hair, styled back behind his ears and wearing a navy-blue suit coat and khaki pants, got out and buttoned his top blazer button. Holly flew through her front doors, past a man carrying some large stainless-steel bowls, and landed in the man's arms. He could hear her call the man 'Daddy'.

The one person she said always had her back was now holding her hands and kissing her cheeks. His presence there had an immediate effect on her demeanor. She bounced on her toes and pointed to her repainted shop sign.

Perhaps the visit was the first time her father had seen all her hard work, and just in time to observe everything coming back together. Theodor couldn't help but wish for his own father or mother to visit his shop too. His father made it clear that he wanted nothing to do with Theodor or his little hobby. His mother, on the other hand, was a quiet supporter when it suited her.

As a child she would pack his little Spiderman wallet with extra spending money when she thought his father didn't think he deserved anything for nothing. His father was a lost hope, but maybe if he asked, his mother would come to his opening in a few days. And if she came, maybe she could see him win the grant money when they made the announcement at the Independence Day festival.

There was no reason Holly should have all the parental support around here, and Theodor had a phone call make.

CHAPTER 25

HOLLY SAT ON THE WARM WOOD OF THE DOCK WITH HER LEGS hanging over the side, rocking the little boat with her bare toes resting on the bow. Up the path from the shore, a light was on inside Teddy's cabin. His shadow would cross in front of his windows every once in a while, like he was pacing back and forth. Anticipation grew for him to come out and meet up with her at any moment, but now it was eight-fifty-nine and Holly was done waiting for life to unfold in its own time.

She stood, slipped her feet into a pair of orange Crocs she had borrowed from Millie, and marched straight down the path to Teddy's. Unsure of what she would say exactly, she slowed her pace and thought it through. The last thing she needed to do was yell at him or scare him off for yet another reason, though her initial idea was to let him have it.

"Hi, Teddy, You're late for our date. Are you getting back at me for being late the other day or because you're avoiding me?" She kicked some of the gravel and paced the other direction. "Hi, Teddy. It's me. No, that's stupid. He'll know it's me when he opens the door. But will he open the door? I don't know."

A light flicked off inside his place and the windows went

dark. It was early for him to go to bed, although they did have a big day tomorrow with the Chamber members evaluations and soft opening. As it was, she still had to go back to her shop and check on the ice cream she had started earlier, so maybe he was turning in early or had forgotten about meeting her at all. She considered that it was selfish for her to have added something more to his plate that night by asking him on a date in the first place. But then why would he just not tell her?

She still didn't have her phone, and supposed it was in her car at the repair shop or flung into a field somewhere. And even though she had been without it for several days, she didn't mind being disconnected. That's what small towns are for. Despite not having a phone, he could have just met with her, a hundred yards from his cabin, and said he was tired and going to sleep. He was avoiding her, just like she suspected.

She practiced what she really wanted to say and what she wanted him to know as she walked the pathway. "Hi, Teddy. I changed my mind about puffins."

"Why's that?" Teddy said from a rocking chair on his front porch and nearly caused her skin to jump off her body.

Her heart pounded in her chest, and she covered the most violent spot with her palm. "You scared me half to death. Where did you come from?"

"I heard someone outside my room talking and came out to see what was going on. I was surprised to see you out here pacing and chatting to yourself," Teddy said and rocked his seat.

She approached with caution. "How much did you hear?"

"What about puffins, Blake Holly Hollis?"

Now that she was on the spot, and clearly not in control of this interaction, she didn't want to tell him. She hesitated to answer until she stood at the bottom of his steps. "Well, everyone knows how cute they are, that's obvious." She stepped up one stair. "They're docile, which some people might think is a drawback, but you see ..." she stepped up one more tread and he stood from his seat. She was three feet away and could already smell the thick scent of cocoa emanating from him. It was an aroma she wanted to wrap herself with.

"What do you want me to see, Blake Holly Hollis?" he closed the distance between them. Towering above her, he planted his feet on the edge of the landing just in front of her on the first step. The low light didn't stop him from exploring her eyes.

Weakness struck her legs, and she wanted to crumple into his arms. Instead, he gave her a hand and she took it. He pulled her up. They stood toe-to-toe. "You see, puffins are docile, but they will fight viciously to protect what's theirs."

"How do you know that?" Teddy asked.

"It's important to study the enemy so you know their weaknesses."

"And I'm the enemy?"

She shook her head. "How can you be the enemy when I would do anything to keep you?"

"You mean, you would fight to have me to yourself?" He brushed her hair away from her cheek the way she knew he liked to do.

She leaned her face into his warm palm. "What do you think I'm doing here? I want you ... to come with me?" She tugged on his hand and headed down the steps. He pulled back and stopped her half-way down. "You really don't want to do this, do you?"

"I don't know, Holly. One minute I feel like our hearts are speaking the same language, like we're two magnets drawn close. And the next, I don't know what to think. My mind can't reconcile with my heart."

"That's fair," she said because she felt the same way. "If I could go back and undo what I did, I would ... Or maybe I wouldn't."

"What do you mean?"

"Think about it. Without all this strife, would I be as clear as I am now about what I want? And I'm not just talking about you. I'm talking about being the kind of person that I can be proud of, not worrying about what my parents think. It's not important how I got to this point, but it is important that I got here. And here I am, standing in front of the man that I've gotten here with."

He was quiet and unmoving. She had no choice but to wait for him to say something. Was her confession enough? She could feel tension increase in his fingers against her hand squeezing her like a vice. If he applied any more pressure, they would risk being fused together. Forever. "Say something."

"So, you're saying you want me?" he smirked, his teeth glinting off the ambient light of the solar lanterns lining the path.

"Really?" she giggled. "That's what you got from all that? You're such a boy."

He let that one slide and stepped down one below her. "Where did you want to take me?"

She smiled knowing what she had planned. What he had almost missed out on. She led him to the boat tied up on the side of the dock. He got into the small wooden rowboat first and helped her in next. Sitting across from him, the sliver of moon reflected little ripples of light around the water's surface. Teddy untied the rope and took the oars.

"Where to?"

"Our spot," she said and grinned.

Teddy rowed the short distance towards the secluded little section surrounded by low trees and wild bushes. The water was still, but for the tiny waves caused by the oars and the rocking of the boat. He propped an oar against the shallow lakebed like an anchor and the boat came to a stop.

From behind her, she pulled out a small soft-sided cooler. She had almost gone with a basket, but since they were now an hour late for the date, she was glad she had no other choice. She handed him a spoon and a cloth napkin for his lap and put one over her own legs. Shaking the cold melted ice from the glass container, Holly popped off the plastic lid and presented the contents to Teddy.

"What's this?" he said and dipped his spoon in.

"I wanted to show you what I'm so passionate about, since you've shared your gift with me. I figured it was time for you to experience mine." She dipped her spoon in and took a large scoop of ice cream.

"Poison?"

"Just try it." The ice cream hit her tongue. She savored the cool refreshing flavor, but she kept an eye on Teddy's face. "See. Not poison."

He brought the spoonful to his lips before putting the ice cream in his mouth. She hadn't told him the variety, because she wanted him to experience it without bias. He moaned at the flavor warming against his tongue, and she bit her lip as the anticipation subsided.

"I knew you would like it."

He finished his bite and took another. "Spiced mandarin with dark chocolate shavings?"

"I was hoping I could feature a local chocolate in the next batch though. Do you know anyone around here I could use?" she baited him.

"I might know someone." He took another bite. "This is spectacular. I get the smooth creaminess with a bite from the cinnamon, and is that cayenne, too?"

"Just enough for a kick."

"I like it," he said and licked his upper lip from corner to corner. She was sure he was thinking about biting something other than the ice cream.

They both dipped back into the rapidly thawing ice cream and their spoons clinked together causing them to laugh. They savored what was likely the last bite before the contents would need to be sipped instead of scooped. Holly put her spoon in the half-empty glassware and Teddy copied her example.

An uncomfortable tension fell on them. She couldn't think of a time when there was an a more awkward silence. Maybe it was because there were plenty of unsaid things thickening the atmosphere between them. She didn't want to speak and blurt out something else embarrassing, so she cleared her throat.

"Thank you for sharing this with me. Now I feel bad for making you work so hard to get me out here."

At that, she whacked him good. "You mean, you were teasing me, and you were always planning to meet me tonight?"

"To be honest, I wasn't sure about anything until ..."

"Until what, Teddy," she said in a soft tone.

"You told me about how you've changed, and I know what you mean, because I've changed too. I realized that all those people who I felt like I had to have in my corner were all there for a purpose. They pushed me. You pushed me. But I also know that some of those people just aren't going where I'm going."

"Like my mother. Without all of her manipulation and interfering, I don't know if I couldn't have reached the point where I know exactly what I want and what I deserve. I also know how hard I'll work for it."

"How viciously you'll fight to keep what's yours?"

"Precisely. I'm only sorry I had to be so awful to you to see it for myself."

"Oh, honey, I'm not," Teddy said and brushed her lips with the back of his finger. "I've enjoyed every second seeing you become this woman. My woman."

"If you'll have me?" she said and closed her eyes as he slid the back of his hand down her neck. A shiver ran through her like every word he spoke kissed her skin. She pressed her lips together in anticipation of his lips caressing hers.

He flicked his tongue against her mouth and caused her lips to part enough for the night air to cool the wet flesh. He was close enough to taste, and she didn't let him tease her again. She bit back, crashing her lips against his like a hammer hitting its target. This kiss was different than the others, less possessive and more tender. It was as though their lips were doing all the talking their hearts wanted and not their brains.

His hands were on her body, mapping her curves and exploring her reaction to him. He knelt in front of her in the boat, peppering kisses down the length of her neck. The sudden change of weight rocked the boat side to side. The kisses continued until their laughter overtook their connection. They both gripped the sides of the boat not wanting to end up in the water.

"Whoa! Teddy!" she yelled through a laugh.

He moved his bottom back to the narrow bench and used the oars to calm the swaying. "Maybe we should head back. We both have a big day tomorrow."

"Hey, Teddy. Whatever happens with the grant money, I want you to know that I think you have something special. And I know it'll work out either way," Holly said.

"I want you to win. Not just the money, but the bet."

"The bet?" She had nearly memory-holed the wager they made all those weeks ago. "If you win, I have to stock your candies in my shop. And if I win—"

"You get to take me on a real date," Teddy said, and she could tell he was smirking.

"Does tonight count?"

He rowed around to the end of the dock and the moon illuminated his face. "Not even close."

CHAPTER 26

THEODOR RAN HIS FINGERS THROUGH HIS HAIR IN A FUTILE EFFORT to fight against the wind whipping around to the back of the pickup truck where he sat. He was minutes away from seeing Holly, and later they would learn who won the grant money. He hadn't seen much of Holly since their ice cream date in the boat. The day afterwards, the Chamber of Commerce had their walk-through during the soft opening. The most he had seen of her was a smile or a friendly wave from their respective shop windows.

He was impressed that her space had been ready in time for the review at all, though he suspected the majority of the work to fix what the fire had damaged was geared towards the forward-facing elements of her business and not the behind-the-scenes areas. In addition to the countless workers, Holly's father had also made several more appearances which only made him long to have his own parents' support. The last two weeks had shown him he could manage without his family's assistance. His savings would be enough to get him through the next month until his shop was making an income. Though he didn't need anything from them now, he still desired, like any child does, to win their approval.

This weekend was the last peaceful time he would have before his dream of being a full-time chocolatier could come true. He could practically taste his impending success, and it tasted so sweet his mouth watered. He'd come a long way in the past few weeks, not only with a boost of confidence in his life choices, but also letting his heart have a louder voice in his decision making. He smiled at his wingman, Alfonso, sitting beside him in the bed of the truck.

"Why so happy, bro?" Alfonso asked with his own goofy grin splashed across his face.

The truck pulled up to the corner on Main and came to a stop. "Blake Holly Hollis, that's why," Theodor said and jumped out of the bed of Leo's red pickup alongside Alfonso. His feet hit the cobblestones, and he brushed any dirt or bits of straw from his bottom that he might have picked up during the short trip. Riding in the back of Leo's vehicle was preferable to walking into town in this heat, even if it were in the exposed bed with only a horse blanket to sit on.

Alfonso patted Theodor's back, and they stepped up to the sidewalk. "Millie drives Holly tonight."

"I know." Theodor came around the truck. He opened the passenger door and helped America out. Leaning in the doorway, he thanked Leo for the lift.

"Don't mention it," Leo said. "We were already headed this way. Do you need a ride back after the fireworks later?"

Theodor waved him off. "It'll be cooled down enough to walk."

"Good luck tonight," America said. "You think you'll win the grant?"

"I have as good a chance as anyone else. All the owners have worked so hard, and I think that Main Street is better for it," Theodor said wondering if he really had a good chance.

"I think you're right," Leo said. "When I was mayor, I never would have considered that a friendly competition could have had such a big impact on the whole town. I'll have to thank … the anonymous benefactor later."

Theodor placed his hands on the hood of the truck. "You know who it is? Who's giving the money?"

Leo zipped his mouth shut and patted Theodor square on his back as he came around to America's side. "I can't say, but you'll find out tonight for sure."

Theodor wished he had known who it was this whole time and could have sucked up or sidled up. "Thanks again for the ride. Have fun, you two."

"You too," America said and pointed at Theodor and then Alfonso. "Be good."

Theodor chuckled in his throat. Alfonso was no doubt his best friend in town, and if he was totally honest, the Italian was probably the most loyal friend he had ever had. It was a relationship Theodor knew he needed in his life. He threw his arm over Alfonso's shoulder, and they walked onto Main where the festivities were already in full swing and where he knew he would find Holly.

Groups of families and friends all moved in the same direction towards the old city hall. Above him, string lights hung between the building rooflines, and red, white, and blue bunting decorated each light post lining the road. All of Main Street screamed Fourth of July with patriotic streamers and wreaths adorning every corner.

All of the existing businesses were open. The little boutique had a constant stream of shoppers coming and going. A food truck, smoking some barbeque, had set up in front of an empty storefront. Down by his shop, a young man stood below a shade structure making balloon animals for the kids. Another shade tent housed a woman who was painting children's faces with flags and butterflies.

A kid ran by, bumping Theodor's elbow, and then another child pushed between him and Alfonso while brandishing a balloon sword and wearing a balloon pirate hat. "Reminds me of a Hallmark movie," Theodor commented as he scanned the crowd for Holly's unmistakable golden ponytail.

"What is Hallmark movie?" Alfonso said.

Theodor had only ever watched one a few years ago. "When I had my wisdom teeth out, my grandma and I binged-watched a bunch of movies. It's an American TV channel that plays these cheesy movies and shows that are so not realistic, but the stories show a kind of life that I think we all long for. A happy one."

"*Si. Rai Movie* in *Italia* same. Alfonso like the kissy kissy *amore*." He made the smooching sound towards Theodor's cheeks and swiftly took an elbow to the ribs.

"Look, look, look," Theodor said and stopped in his tracks, pulling Alfonso to a stop beside him and patting his chest.

The crowd parted just enough for him to see the hottest women in town walking down the sidewalk towards them. Millie wore a white button-down shirt tucked into a pair of tiny denim shorts. She was cute, but Holly was … "Gorgeous."

Her hips swayed back and forth along with her ponytail. A fluffy blue ribbon floated on the breeze behind her head, and little red crystals glittered on the straps of her heels. She wore a skin hugging white dress with red and blue sequin stars dotting the surface. The whole Miss America ensemble left little to his feverish imagination.

"Go get your woman," Theodor said to Alfonso who wasted no time jogging ahead towards Millie.

The action got Millie's attention, and Holly searched the crowd of faces for a second before her gaze fell on him. She stopped and smiled while preforming a little curtsy. Theodor swirled his finger in the air, and she did a little twirl with her hands held out by her hips. When she came all the way around, she kicked up her heel and tilted her head like a little girl showing off her new outfit and it was the best thing he'd seen in days, since their boat ride. The Chamber had done their inspection a couple days ago, and he hadn't seen her since, though he'd looked across the street dozens of times.

The wait was worth it. He liked seeing her all fixed up, but he had also enjoyed seeing her in her red one-piece bathing suit and matching linen shorts that she wore on their ice cream date. He watched as she whispered something to Millie and skipped the short distance to where he had stopped, halting only when her body collided with his.

Holly reached up on her toes and kissed his cheek with her pillowy soft lips. "Look at this." She backed away, raised a brow, and started scrambling her hands over the little stars on her dress. The red sequins flipped to gold and the blue sequins flipped and became silver. Her face lit up with excitement at the trick.

"How long have you been waiting to show someone this dress?"

"Longer than I want to admit," she said with wide eyes, waiting for approval. "I thought you'd appreciate the flair."

He kissed her nose. "It's adorable." He pecked her lips. "And so are you."

Theodor took her right hand and held it high over her head, leading her into a twirl like a dance. "You might as well be Miss Independence Day in this dress. All you're missing is a crown." He had an idea and, with Holly in tow behind him, hastened towards the young man twisting balloons under the shade tent. He leaned in, cutting in front of a few patient children, and asked for a crown for Holly.

"What are we doing?" she said and giggled nervously. "I don't need a sword or a poodle or whatever he's making."

Theodor placed a finger against her painted red lips and watched the boy go to work with a pair of golden balloons the length of his arm. He twisted and manipulated the rubber to within an inch of its life, and after what didn't seem like enough time to create such a masterpiece, the boy presented Holly with a grand tiara. Theodor handed the boy a few bucks and fit the crown onto Holly's head.

"My princess," he said and bowed.

A little girl, maybe four years old, pulled on Holly's arm and she squatted down to the girls' level. "Are you a real princess?" Her clear eyes were opened wide with a smile to match.

"I am today. And you can be one too." Holly removed the crown and stuck it on the girl's head. "There, now you look like a princess too. All you have to do is be a kind person and hold your head up high."

The girl turned to her father and pointed her finger at his face. "Bow down to me, servant," she demanded, causing Holly to bite her lips between her teeth to stifle the giggle threatening to escape her throat.

"I tried." Holly turned around and finally let out the laugh. "I have a surprise for you." She led him down the sidewalk, not in a hurry, but determined.

He didn't care where she took him, so long as they were going together. He walked just behind her, as the sidewalk was packed with crowds. It would have been nice to open his shop with all the extra foot traffic, but as it was, the final health inspection was scheduled for the first Monday of the month. In this case, he and Holly had to wait through the holiday weekend.

By the look of her in her star-spangled dress, she was making the most of the waiting. As she snaked through the crowd, the setting sun dipped below the rooflines. The shade cut the outside temperatures by what felt like half at least, and his skin relaxed into what promised to be a merry evening. For one thing, he could watch her ponytail swing back and forth all night.

They approached the fountain end of the street, and the air filled with the sounds of a live band. The woman on stage began to sing, accompanied by a single acoustic guitar. Theodor leaned over Holly's shoulder and whispered, "Dance with me."

At his request, she turned around, right into Theodor's arms. His arm casually circled around to her lower back, and he moved his hips in time with the music towards the dance floor set up in the middle of the road. They joined several other couples and some kids swaying to the song. He shouldn't have been surprised that she was eager to follow his lead, but he was.

Her body became part of his as he led her around the floor in an improvised dance. She responded to every subtle command of his hand and every suggestion of his body. They moved as one, making an entire loop until the song ended. Using his arm as a brace, he dipped her backwards, her hair fell and exposed her beautiful long neck to him. He would have liked to kiss her then, but he would reserve the delight for a later time when they weren't surrounded by throngs of complete strangers.

He brought her upright and the crowd clapped for their little display. "I didn't know you could dance like that," Theodor said in a low voice.

"Me?" she said and clapped along with the others. "What about you? That was amazing."

"All those years of ballroom classes weren't for nothing." He winked and took her off the dance floor to where he was pretty sure he sniffed the thick, sugary scent of a fried dough treat. He searched the various stalls and found the one he was looking for but remembered he had sidetracked her to have that dance. "Before I change your plans again, what was that surprise?"

She jumped up and down. "I almost forgot. Come on. I don't know how I could forget this. I want to introduce you to my dad."

"Wait, wait. Your dad is here?" He looked down at his outfit. "Do I look okay?" Why was his heart racing and why were his hands clammy with moisture? He had met a million people in his life. Shaking hands with strangers was a skill he had mastered since childhood. But this wasn't any stranger, this was her father.

The only thing he knew about the man was how much he loved his daughter, but he supposed anyone who could love that much wasn't so scary.

"You look great. You look like a man who is confident with who you are and knows what you want in life," she said and straightened his shirt collar.

"And how do you know what I want, Blake Holly Hollis?" he said.

"Because we want the same things. To make our own choices, and our own mistakes—"

"Wrong." Theodor leaned into her cheek. "I only want you." His lips pressed agonizingly slowly against the apple of her cheek. This wasn't a new revelation; he had wanted her since the day she stared at him on the train. Only now, he had a real chance at happiness with her.

"I knew that too," she said and pecked him on the lips before turning in her heels and walking away.

"Tease!" he yelled above the blaring music.

"Flirt!" she yelled back. They had each other figured out alright. "You coming, or what?"

Did he have a choice? He had a father to meet.

Up ahead, she stopped in front of the man Theodor had seen visiting the creamery over the past week. He was tall with an athletic build, albeit with the slightly slumped shoulders of an older gentleman. He wore a cream linen suit with brown leather loafers like he was on the Amalfi coast, not some small upstate, New England town. But the man looked good.

Holly arched up on her toes and kissed her dad's cheek. She was saying something with a broad smile and some hand clapping. She bounced the way she always did when she was really happy, and Theodor's heart swelled knowing that her light spirit was because of him. He hadn't officially asked her for anything, but with what they had been through, there was no mistaking that they were each other's.

She waved to him to hurry up and her father turned around to look at what she was looking at. Without hesitation, he extended a hand and Theodor did the same. A firm handshake and a soft facial expression was the surest way to greet someone.

"Mister Hollis. It's a pleasure to meet you, sir." Theodor knew to keep things formal until given permission to address him otherwise. Pride swelled that this was really happening.

"Theodor Black. It's nice to meet you, and you can call me Glyn." He had a firm grasp and placed his other hand on top of their joined ones. "I have to admit, Holly did not exaggerate when she told me how good looking you are."

"Daddy, stop it," she said and rolled her eyes.

In an effort to tease her a little more, Theodor took the theme further. "Is that right? And how good is good, Holly? Are we talking Greek God status or like David Hasselhoff circa nineteen-ninety-five?"

"What?" she asked, and her high arched brows indicated she had no idea what he was talking about. "Who's David Hassle-whatever?"

"Never mind," he said and chuckled along with Glyn.

"You two can't gang up on me already." Holly pouted. "I forbid it."

"Would you rather we be enemies, or worse, indifferent?" Glyn said. "I can tell this guy makes you happy. And if you're happy, sweetie, then I'm happy."

She kissed Glyn's cheek again. "Thanks, Daddy."

"Plus," Glyn continued. "Anyone is better than that wannabe, Rinaldi. I never liked that guy."

Theodor nodded. He knew only what Holly had told him about her ex, but he did not sound like a stand-up guy. He was a man-boy with too much of his father's money and no sense.

"I still can't believe what mother did at the review. I just don't know what has gotten into her and wanting to stir things up that I had already put to bed. It's not like she doesn't know about the cheating. And she would still want me to be with someone like that?" Holly's voice had gotten higher-pitched with each sentence. "She doesn't even care about me."

Theodor took her face in his hands and locked eyes with her. "Breathe," he whispered and demonstrated three deep inhales. "We have big things to celebrate. Stop worrying about what everyone else thinks." He released her and stood back, holding her hand in the space between them.

"I just wish she could ... I don't know?" she shrugged.

Glyn clapped his hands together once in front of his own stomach. "She does care about you. She just doesn't understand why you don't want to be more like her. She's a wonderful, independent woman who has built her business from scratch while raising a beautiful daughter."

"But that's just it, I am like her. She doesn't want to admit it. The thing is, I just want something different, is all."

Holly's analysis was spot on. She was probably more like her mom than her mom was willing to accept. Theodor, on the other hand, was nothing like either of his parents. His father would never come around to Theodor's choice. He had made it clear from an early age that being a lawyer was the only path he'd ever support him taking.

Becoming a chocolatier wasn't even in the same realm where his father lived. At least his mother was slightly more supportive. Perhaps not supportive, but she would never do anything to intentionally cut him down. He had invited her to the festival but never heard back, and figured it was a slim chance she'd make an appearance anyway. At least he had extended the invitation. Now the ball was in her court.

"Are you staying for the announcement?" Theodor asked Glyn.

"I wouldn't want to miss it. But if you'll excuse me, I spot an old friend by the fried dough stand." Glyn extended his hand to

Theodor again. Taking it, he shook firmly. "Teddy, it's a pleasure. But I've got an eye on you."

"Yes, sir. Enjoy your treat. And make sure to stop in my shop next time you come this way."

"Wouldn't miss it," Glyn said and took Holly in his arms. "You look beautiful tonight. Hang on to this one," he whispered loud enough for Theodor to hear, and winked at him.

The interaction was a little awkward, though Theodor had no reference point for meeting a girlfriend's father. He had dated a few women who were family friends, so was already acquainted with those fathers. And other girls never brought him home. It never bothered him before, but to see Holly's blush spread across her cheeks at how proud she was to have her father getting along with her boyfriend made him feel like the luckiest guy in the world.

"Holly, I think I ..." he paused his words as he spotted his mother coming through the crowd. "... I see my mother."

Holly followed the line of his pointer finger and laughed. "No, way. My mother actually came, too," she said.

"Your mom?" he was confused. His mom was only a few feet from the edge of the dance floor with her unmistakable slicked black hair and whatever Chanel dress she pulled from her closet. She was in a light-hearted conversation with a woman with long, blonde hair wearing blue jeans and a white blouse. The two women laughed at something, both throwing their heads back almost in unison.

"That's your mom?" Theodor asked to make certain. "Because, if it is, she's talking with mine."

Holly's face became a mix of panic and fear. "This can't be good." She swallowed hard and reset her expression to a neutral calm. Redirecting her footsteps, she pushed through the crush of bodies towards the pair. "Mother," she sang. "What are you doing here?"

His mother spotted him and spoke first. "Hello, dear," she said and kissed his cheeks in her typical greeting.

"You didn't tell me you were acquainted with the Blacks," Holly's mother said and kissed her in the same manner. "This must be the infamous Theodor. Your mother and I go way back."

"You do?" he said and searched his mom's eyes for answers. He recognized the slight raise in her right eyebrow as a way to say she'd tell him more later.

"We met at a charity function a few years back. It was the ..."

"I believe it was the Stallion and Stalls gala. We raised several million dollars for equestrian opportunities for troubled youth. It was a wonderful event."

"That's right," Holly's mother said and snapped her fingers. "You can imagine my surprise to find you so far from Manhattan, out here in the sticks."

"Mother. This happens to be our home. It's not like we're in the boonies," Holly said and spoke softly. "Why are you even here? Don't you usually attend the event at the Drayton's?"

"Yes, of course. I'm heading there soon, but I brought you something." She turned to Theodor and his mom. "Excuse me, I have something waiting for Holly. Catch up soon." She took Holly by the hand and moved away from him.

Holly reached back behind, pleading for help, but his own mother turned his attention away.

"The Hollis girl, really?" she said.

"What's wrong with the Hollis girl?" he said with the same affected tone his mom had just used when saying her name.

"She's a troublemaker. Her mother says she's a miscreant and even went to jail. I just hope this isn't the girl that you've been making your questionable life choices for. A pretty face isn't worth throwing away your future." She continued without so much as letting him take a breath. "Your father warned me not to come here, but I thought I would come show you some support. But I'm sorry dear, I can't support this."

"Which part?"

"I beg your pardon?"

"I said, which part? You don't approve of me being a chocolatier or a small business owner? Or you don't approve of a woman I'm falling in love with and who makes me feel seen for the first time in my life. Which is it?"

She huffed and feigned offense. Her hand covered her white pearl necklace. "I will not be spoken to in such a manner. I raised you better than to behave like this."

"That's the thing. You didn't raise me. I raised myself, or grandma did. I did what I was supposed to do. I smiled and nodded. And then I grew up. I'm not sorry I didn't become the lawyer you and dad wanted me to be, but at some point, you'll see that I've become the man you had hoped I would become, just with a different career."

She stood, slack-jawed at his rebuke and shook her head. "I've never ..." her words trailed off at having nothing else to say and walked away.

Now, where was Holly? He suspected his girlfriend needed saving too.

CHAPTER 27

HOLLY LOOKED BACK OVER HER SHOULDER IN TIME TO SEE TEDDY loosening his hair from the knot at the back of his head. She liked his hair down and hanging around his facial hair, adding to the shadow on his jawline. His easy-going style bled into his clothing choices too. He exuded a whole good-boy on Sunday, bad-boy on a dirt bike vibe, and she was here for it.

He turned around, facing the sky, and flung his hands down by his side, while his mother walked away from him. *That was a short visit*, Holly thought. She turned and looked at her mother as they continued moving further from Teddy. She was on a mission, whatever it was, but Holly decided to go see what had caused such distress on Teddy's face.

Holly tugged on her mother's wrist. "Can this wait?" she asked her mother. "I need to go back to Teddy."

Her mother came around and put a hand in the middle of Holly's back, pushing her along. "In a minute. But first, and don't get mad—"

"What are you up to?" Holly rolled her eyes. "Anytime you tell me not to be mad, you know you're about to irritate me, but you hope you lessen the degree by warning me first."

"You don't know everything, Blake. But, in this case, please be nice."

"Who am I being nice to—" she didn't have to finish the thought because Rinaldi stood from a small table at the restaurant by the plaza and put his hands up like he was surrendering. "You've got to be kidding me! Mom, no. I am not in the mood for this right—"

"Just hear him out. Will you?"

Under no circumstance did Holly want to hear anything Rinaldi had to say to her. "Here I was thinking you came here to support me tonight, and instead, you're scheming again." The blood in her veins felt hot and it wasn't from the outside temperature. She was mad.

Rinaldi closed the short distance between them. "Please, baby. Give me five minutes?"

She really didn't want to, but like the day at the club, there were way too many people around and she did not want to make a scene. It was obvious her mother was putting her thumb on the scales again. Holly wondered, as her mother urged her forward with shifting eyes, if she would ever be free of her mother's influence. The band began to play an up-tempo song. "You have until this song is over. No more."

"That's all I need," the snake said.

She wanted to swipe the grin from his face. "Don't push your luck."

He took her right hand in his and trapped her waist with his other, leading her backwards onto the dance floor where several other couples were already dancing.

Millie and Alfonso, engaged in their own dance, passed by. Millie made eye contact. "What is he doing here?" she mouthed.

All Holly could do was shrug. "Time's ticking," she urged Rinaldi.

"You look wonderful, baby," he started but her muscles were already cringing at him calling her baby and complimenting her.

"I guess I'll just come out and say it. I want you back, and I'll do anything to win your trust. I know I was a total cad, the worst boyfriend ever."

"I don't want any excuses—"

"I won't patronize you with some half-hearted justification, but maybe the truth as I saw it."

She didn't interrupt and let him continue as he pushed her around the floor. This dance, unlike the intimate one she had shared with Teddy a little while earlier, was stiff and clumsy, but she did her best to follow his erratic lead.

"When we were in Split. I panicked. I had a plan to surprise you. To proclaim my devotion to you—"

"Cheating on me is a funny way of showing devotion."

"I was calming my nerves—"

"With whisky?"

"Tequila, actually," he shot back. "I was over-served. It wasn't my fault—"

"You accidentally fell in bed with another girl?"

"Will you stop interrupting me?" Rinaldi said, and Holly realized she really hated being told what to do "There's more. I won't lie. Yes, I slept with that woman. She was hot, okay? And I was so drunk I don't even remember how she got to our place. That's beside the point. The reason I was so nervous was because ..."

She searched his tortured face for any clue as to what he was about to reveal. Their breakup had had a clear impact on him, and he was more flustered than she had ever seen. His dark eyes were not the carefree eyes of the man she had dated last year. These orbs were full of regret and humanity. She almost felt bad for him. "The song's almost over."

Rinaldi let her go and took something out of his front pants pocket. Before she could stop him, he was down on one knee in front of her presenting a sparkling princess cut diamond ring to her. "Blake Hollis, I love you. Will you agree to be my wife, my partner, and the other half of my soul? Marry me."

She knew her answer was a resounding *no*, but for some reason, with dozens of eyeballs boring holes into her, she froze. This was not the proposal she had dreamed of recently. *Teddy*, she thought, *I want Teddy*. She inspected the faces in the crowd where she had last seen him, but the dance had turned her around and he wasn't anywhere in that direction. Millie caught her eye and pointed. Holly spun around just in time to see Teddy marching across the dance floor towards them.

Teddy scooped her into his arms like a beast and pressed a possessive kiss on her lips. She would never forget the way he let his whole heart pour into her in that moment. She was full of the kind of love she deserved. He broke the kiss, set her down and pulled Rinaldi to his feet. "You son of a bitch," Teddy growled.

Seeing them standing toe-to-toe, it wasn't even a contest. She'd take the saint any day. Millie came around to Holly's side and put a protective arm around her shoulders as they watched the unfolding altercation between the man she loved and the boy she had left in her past where he belonged.

"Hey man. What the hell? Can't you see I'm proposing to my girl?" Rinaldi attempted to push past Teddy.

In response, Teddy placed his palm on Rinaldi's chest. "Her answer is no. Now get out of here."

"Who the hell are you thinking you can speak for Blake," Rinaldi said and leaned his head around Teddy's broad body to see her face. "Does he chew your food too, baby?"

That was it! Holly marched right up to Rinaldi and slapped him across the face. Her hand stung like it had been pricked by thousands of tiny pins and needles, and she shook the pain off. "It's none of your business if he does or doesn't. My answer is always going to be no. Now get out of here, you snake."

"You brat!" he lurched forward towards her, and she narrowly dodged his attempt to grab her arm.

Teddy shoved him backwards and Alfonso and Millie stood on either side of Teddy like a wall. Holly's heart, though it was beating faster than she thought was possible, was full of gladness for the friend group she now had.

Millie stuck her pointer and middle finger in Rinaldi's' direction and taunted him to advance again. "Try it, and find out," she said.

Rinaldi began to back off and Holly's mother came through the crowd. Instead of checking on her own daughter, she took Rinaldi's shoulders in her hands and asked if he was alright. He put his head on her shoulder, and she stroked the man's hair.

A warm hand rested on Holly's shoulder, and she turned to see who it might be. "Daddy," she said and hugged her father. "Did you see what she did?"

"She's gone too far this time," he said and stood back.

"I can't do this anymore with her. I'm tired of being under her thumb and this was the last straw." She hugged her dad again.

"I didn't realize," her father said. "With all the traveling and … It's no excuse. I'll take care of it."

For the first time, Holly felt like she wasn't imagining her mother's actions. Everyone around the dance floor, including her father, saw it too. A few weeks ago, Holly would have been way more bothered by her mother's disloyalty, but now, as she smiled at her friends, and the man who had her heart, she didn't even care. Rinaldi and her mother exited the dance floor, the previous song having long ended.

The band started up another tune, an instrumental version of *I Hope You Dance*, one of Holly's favorites. This time she wanted to take control. "Saint Teddy," this time she called him that with no hint of sarcasm. "Will you do me the honor of dancing with me?"

He said no words. Just approached her and took her in his arms. Her feet didn't hit the floor again for several breaths. In his hold, he spun her around and took her mouth with his. His facial hair rubbed against her lips and sent a thrill through her. Not one of their other kisses had been so romantic. If they weren't in public, with practically the entire town staring at them, she might have let down her hair, but the reality was they had appearances to uphold as business owners.

She pulled away and he placed her down on her tip toes when the microphone screeched from the stage. They paused and stood side by side. Teddy threaded his fingers through hers and she squeezed tight. It was time for the announcement.

Up on the stage, a man, no more than forty tapped his fingers on the mic. The crowd quieted and some people pushed forward to be closer to the front. From their place at the center of the dance floor, Holly could see just fine, and hearing the overpowered mic was not a problem.

"Happy Independence Day, folks," the man started. "For those of you who don't know me. I'm Mayor Thorpe and if this isn't the biggest Fourth of July festival we've ever had, call me a monkey's uncle. Who here is having a good time? Let me hear you say 'fireworks'!"

The crowd responded with shouts and clapping, eliciting a giggle. There was far too much joy in the air to be mad about Rinaldi or her mother. She leaned into Teddy. "Whatever happens?"

"Whatever happens," he repeated and nudged her with his shoulder.

Mayor Thorpe hushed the crowd with his hands. "Now, before we can get to the big show here in a little bit, I believe some of our business owners are waiting for an announcement."

A woman who Holly had met briefly at the girls' night came across the stage. The older woman held a white envelope in her hand and tapped the end of the mic. "Hello, Christmas Cove!" she shouted, and the crowd cheered. "My name is Carol. Many of you know me and know that I've loved this town for a very long time. A few months back, I married the love of my life, Pa, right here in town. As it turns out, before my father passed away many years ago, he set up a trust that only paid out if I ever got married. The thing is, I avoided marriage for so long because of him." Carol looked at an older man, Holly assumed was her husband, and he encouraged her to keep going with a smile.

Carol gave a nervous giggle in her throat. "The irony. Anyway, I don't need all that money, and thought, what better way to celebrate the town I love than to help get Main Street back up and kicking again." She put her hand out towards Pa, and he joined her on stage. "We decided to award fifty-thousand dollars to a most deserving establishment."

Pa stepped to the mic. "And to all the applicants, we are paying three months of your rent."

This announcement alone created an uproarious applause. Holly grabbed Teddy's arm. "Isn't this great?"

He nodded as Pa began speaking again. "Okay, okay, folks. The winner of the fifty-thousand dollars is ..." The band's drummer started his sticks on the snare drum. "Cove Candles. Congratulations. Let's give a round of applause to owner, Angela Catsberry."

Shoot, Holly thought and looked up at Teddy's face. His puckered lips and deep breath showed his disappointment, but she wasn't sad.

"Are you upset?" he asked.

"No, because I think I already won," she said and threw her arms around his shoulders. Teddy challenged her to be a better person. He was the man who would protect her, encourage her, and love her no matter what. "Teddy—"

"I love you, too," he said and crushed his lips against hers again. His passion caused her to melt into him. He was her puffin, viciously fighting for what was his. She hoped she could earn his loyalty every day, and starting now, she would ensure she was worthy of his love. The good thing is, neither of them were in a hurry to leave the Cove, to start over anywhere else or with anyone else. They had time on their side and the support of their true friends.

She looked over and saw Millie and Alfonso going at it, lip to lip. "Look, look," she said to Teddy, breaking their own connection.

"To be young and in love," he said and winked. She intertwined her fingers with his and stood back. "Does this mean I'm your girlfriend now?"

"Oh, honey, you're my everything. Now let's enjoy this firework show." He guided her to a stone bench surrounding the fountain.

They sat down, her head rested on his shoulder, and they watched the sparkling colors explode overhead just like the bangers lighting up in her heart. She might have taken the long and bumpy tracks to get there, but no other way would have been as exciting a ride. "I love you, Teddy Black."

RATE AND REVIEW

We hope you enjoyed *Sweet Summertide* by Sarah Dressler. If you did, we would ask that you please rate and review this title. Every review helps our authors.

Rate and Review: Sweet Summertide - Book 4

MEET THE AUTHOR

Sarah Dressler is a Florida gal who traded her sunshine state for the snowy peaks of Colorado! From fashionista and blogger to full-time fiction writer, Sarah's pen never rests. Don't be fooled, she's no homebody; this globe-trotting adventurer is a military brat turned military spouse. When she's not spinning tales, she's strolling into the sunset with her hubby of two decades or chasing after her pair of energetic teens.

OTHER TITLES FROM

5 PRINCE PUBLISHING

www.5princebooks.com
New to Newport *Emi Hilton*
Trusting the Alpha *Courtney Davis*
Sweet Summertide *Sarah Dressler*
No Words After I Love You *S.E. Reichert*
The Rocking of the Ocean *Barbara Matteson*
Demons and Tea Leaves *Courtney Davis*
Shadow of the Throne *Russell Archey*
Shadow Among the Stars *Courtney Davis*
The Pack *E.C. Saulness*
Keeping Kama *Emi Hilton*
A Winter's Wedding *Sarah Dressler*
Trimutant *April Marcom*
Soul Sacrifice *Courtney Davis*
Picking Pismo *Emi Hilton*
The Taste of Treachery *Emily Bybee*
Spring Showers *Sarah Dressler*
Secret Admirer Pact *Bernadette Marie*
The Publicity Stunt *Bernadette Marie*
A Trace of Romance *Ann Swann*